Okay. It may only be the end  but I, Prudence Stewart, am making my ___ tions early. It's crunch time, and I don't have any more squirm room.

First resolution: Stop wishing I wasn't a witch. Cold turkey on that one.

I know I'm a witch. I may not have manifested that darned Talent that all the other witches have manifested by my age. But I will. I know it just the same way I knew I would get boobs eventually. And I did (the real kind too, not silicone like some of my more impatient former classmates).

But I'm having trouble doing the "just say no" thing to practically everything I've ever known and done my whole mortal life. Solution? A new, uber-self-disciplined Pru.

I had to study 24/7 to pass my classes before? Fine. I'll make it 48/14 for my new schedule of regular magic classes. No problem.

Agatha, the headmistress of the school, hates me because my mortal ways are disruptive? And maybe a little because her great-great-great-great-grandson Daniel ran away right after kissing me? Okay. I'll show her I'm the best little witch in the world.

My cheerleading team doesn't get what it takes to win a national competition? Fine. I'll make them listen if I have to use a hair straightener as a weapon . . . or an incentive.

Boys? My luck is bound to change on that score. . . .

She's a
Witch
Girl

KELLY McCLYMER

Simon Pulse
New York London Toronto Sydney

SIMON PULSE
An imprint of Simon & Schuster Children's Publishing Division
1230 Avenue of the Americas, New York, NY 10020
Copyright © 2007 by Kelly McClymer
All rights reserved, including the right of reproduction in whole or
in part in any form.
SIMON PULSE and colophon are registered trademarks of
Simon & Schuster, Inc.
Designed by Ann Zeak
The text of this book was set in Berthold Garamond.
Manufactured in the United States of America
First Simon Pulse edition August 2007
10 9 8 7 6 5 4 3 2 1
Library of Congress Control Number 2007923035
ISBN-13: 978-1-4169-4902-2
ISBN-10: 1-4169-4902-X

To Jim, who taught me that competition
can occasionally be enjoyable and rewarding.

Acknowledgments
Thanks to Nadia, Michelle, Beth, and all the amazing
behind-the-scenes crew at Simon & Schuster. Without all of your
help, this book wouldn't have been as easy or fun for me to write.

SHE'S A
Witch
Girl

Chapter 1

Maybe it isn't wise to combine witches and mortals at the holiday dinner table, but my family has been a mix-and-match family for as long as I can remember and everyone still seems happy to be invited. Even the half that doesn't believe in magic or think witches really exist. At least everybody—even my grandfather the master warlock—shows up, eats, and says the same lame things families say on holidays. Things like, "You look great." Or, "We shouldn't wait so long to get together." Some things never change.

But some things do. I used to hope my bratty little brother Tobias, aka the Dorklock, would try casting a spell in front of our mortal relatives. That way, I'd get to see what happened and he'd get in trouble. He never paid attention to the "no magic" rule we used to have, even when we lived like mortals back in Beverly Hills.

Everything except the relatives around the table is different this year. We live in Salem, Massachusetts, now. We can do magic. And Dorklock turned out to be gifted and talented at magic. Now he's the golden child and I'm the one on gold-plate probation, fresh from the humiliation of remedial magic classes.

For the three months Dorklock had been learning to charm his way to the top of his class for the first time ever, I'd only managed to scrape my way out of remedial classes. Technically, I hadn't even yet had a regular magic class—that would have to wait until after the Thanksgiving break. Thankfully, no one could congratulate me on my success, since it was a secret from the mortal half of the family and Mom had made sure to cast a superstrong magic damping spell over the entire house. Not that Grandmama and Grandfather couldn't get around one of my mom's spells. But chances were good they would behave themselves this year. They thought they had won mega-points over my mortal grandparents when the whole family made the move to Salem and started doing magic full time. Except my dad, of course, who is mortal and couldn't so much as summon a feather from half an inch away.

"I'll do the dishes for you for a week if there's no big blowout this year," the Dorklock had offered as we sat neatly groomed waiting for the grandmothers to arrive and pinch our cheeks and tell us how sweet we were. Gag me.

Being a big sister meant knowing when it was important to ask, "What do you want from me if there is?"

"You do the dishes and the garbage." He grinned, like the brat he was, daring me to take the bet.

I noticed right away that advantage was to him. Doing the dishes was a magic task, but taking out the trash involved carting the trashcan to the street the mortal way, just in case the neighbors noticed. Still, I said, "You're on." He'd always been sneaky, but even though our situation had changed, Mom and Dad were probably going to keep the magic slippage under control. They've had lots of experience keeping mortals in the dark about the fact that three-quarters of our family can do magic.

Sure, we've had a few unexpected but very necessary mind-wipes when my mom's witch relatives had a little too much of the holiday cheer to drink and my dad's mortal family saw something that gave them the equivalent of brain-freeze. But my parents juggled tricky incidents like a pair of Cirque du Soleil pros.

Take, for example, the rules they've worked out. First, we only host mixed gatherings on holidays. Second, we serve hors d'oeuvres at two, dinner at three, and hand out doggie bags promptly at eight. Apparently, at their wedding reception, my parents discovered that any longer than six hours and the likelihood of a magic-mortal disaster shot up. The "unfortunate occurrence," as my parents obliquely refer to the incident, must have been a good story, because they told us their rules but they never told us what happened to prompt the six-hour limit. Even Grandmama won't talk about it. One day I hope to worm the story out of Dad. If he sticks around, that is, instead of taking off like my ex–best friend Maddie's dad back in Beverly Hills.

When we first moved here, I thought Mom and Dad might be heading for splitsville. I was having so much trouble adjusting to my new school, Dad even threatened to move back to Beverly Hills and take me with him. We'd lived on Dad's side of the mortal-witch divide for, well, ever. His adjustment to the new anything-magic-goes policy had been almost as bumpy as my starting at the bottom of the social ladder at Agatha's Day School for Witches.

In the end, we stayed. I got better at figuring out the witch stuff—not a lot better, but my success-graph does have a slight upward trend right now, and I guess Dad's did too.

Watching him stand at the head of the holiday table carving the turkey, you'd never guess he ever had a doubt about the move. He was pretty cheerful as he forked perfect slices of turkey onto the corny turkey-shaped plate he always used on Thanksgiving. "I just want to thank everyone for joining us for our first Thanksgiving in Salem." He looked pointedly at Dorklock and then at me as he went on. "I hope you two realize how very fitting it is that we get to celebrate this holiday in the place where the Pilgrims lived."

He had that "deep thought" look in his eye. Like he was saying something profound that only Tobias and I could understand. I looked at my friend Samuel, who was sitting next to me, and rolled my eyes.

Samuel didn't play. So typical. He was a mortal-groupie and thought everything Dad said was brilliant. Plus, he and his dad were invited guests at our family table, and Samuel does have good manners for a witch-geek extraordinaire.

"Sure, Dad," the Dorklock agreed. Of course he did. He's the golden child in Salem. And I almost forgot to mention the other rule for holidays was that we were always supposed to agree all day long, no matter what. If Grandma Edna asked if we were doing well in school, we nodded in agreement. If Dad asked if we were having fun, another nod.

Toward the end of the six hours it sometimes got hairy. In the past, I'd managed to avoid breaking the rule by sneaking to my room for a quick scream-fest into my pillow: "No, I do not want another helping of sweet potato. No! That hat you're wearing makes you look like a 'fashion-don't' poster. No! I am not having fun!"

I have no idea how Dorklock survived the holiday yes-fest. For all I knew, he may have created an ever-nodding dopplegänger and escaped off to his video games.

Unfortunately, I didn't feel like being so agreeable this

year. Sure, I'm on the cheerleading team, and I just managed to get out of remedial magic classes by some miracle. But I'm so far away from where I'd have been in Beverly Hills that I just can't get into the whole "being thankful" thing this year. I didn't look at Samuel when I asked my dad, with my patented false-innocence smile, "Which side are the Indians and which side are the Pilgrims?"

Fortunately, before Dad could get mad, everyone laughed. So he moved on to the moment I was dreading most. Picture this: In addition to Samuel and his dad, there are twelve of us (Mom, Dad, me, Dorklock, Grandmama, Grandfather, and Cousin Mike on the witch side; Grandma Edna, Aunt Sylvia, Aunt Donna, her husband, Steve, and their son, Scotty, on the mortal side). The food is steaming on the table in front of us. Our glasses are filled with sparkling cider or champagne, depending on age and preference. Our plates are full. Dad puts the carving knife down, lifts his glass of champagne, and everyone gets quiet, waiting for the inevitable speech about how wonderful it is to have the whole family gathered together yet again.

Dad even gave that tradition a Salem twist this year. "I can almost imagine that there were Pilgrims on this very spot, gathered as we are today. Let us take just a moment to thank them for all they built for us."

While everyone else did the obligatory head bow, I looked at the ghosts who lived in the house, who were standing around the table watching the spectacle of the living. There were several dressed in the never-going-to-be-fashionable Pigrim style. They definitely approved of this year's sentiment. I think they were especially touched by Dad's words because they knew he couldn't see them. It almost made the corny tradition seem normal—at least as normal as possible for a half-witch, half-mortal family.

After a second, Dad looked at Samuel's dad. "Matthias, we are glad you and Samuel could join us. I'd like you to start off the family tradition of going around the table and saying what each of us are grateful for this year."

Oh, goody. Despite the ghosts of Pilgrims past standing there, I didn't look forward to the traditional thanks merry-go-round any better this year than I ever had. It seemed so fake. Take, for example, Samuel's dad giving thanks for being invited to our table. Dude, I hoped that wasn't the highlight of his year. I tried to catch Samuel's eye to apologize for the dork-overload, but he was looking at my dad. I only had about a nanosecond of embarrassment-alert before he lifted his glass of sparkling apple cider to take his turn. "I'm grateful that Pru came to my school this year and I found a great new friend."

I couldn't believe he'd actually said that. I gave him a swift kick under the table for the ten seconds of surround-sound "ahs" and the double dose of grandmotherly laser vision he'd brought down on us.

Fortunately, Mom gave her thanks and took all the attention away from us. "I'm thankful that I've just accepted a position as interim librarian at Agatha's School for . . . um"–she looked at me–"girls . . ." She looked at Samuel. "And . . . um . . . boys."

"Excellent!" said Grandma Edna, Aunt Sylvia, and Aunt Donna. They were strong believers in women not being entirely dependent on a man. If they knew how independent Mom was, I think they might have agreed with Grandmama and Grandfather, who both looked appalled as they said, "A job?"

I didn't hear what anyone else was thankful for because my head was buzzing with the horror of my mother getting a job at Agatha's. Which was a school for witches, not girls . . . and . . . um . . . boys. Oh, wait, I did tune in for Dorklock's thanks: "I'm glad Mom got a job at Pru's school and not mine." Brat.

I know a cheerleader should have a better attitude. But things had changed so much this year already that I was actually most grateful I still looked like me when I checked myself out in the mirror. So was it any wonder that when it was my turn to be thankful for something that I raised my glass of bubbly cider and said, "I'm thankful I haven't failed anything. Yet."

My dad cleared his throat and gave me a look. But I was safe from a lecture with everyone at the table. "My turn, then." Dad lifted his glass again and said, "To my wife, who has put together an amazing feast, as usual. To Tobias, who found a pair of clean socks for the occasion." He paused while everyone laughed. I could see the look in his eye, so I knew to brace for what was coming next. "And to Pru, who has adjusted to her new school with her usual grace." He ignored my scowl and smiled at everyone around the table. "Now, to quote the Pilgrims at the first feast: 'Let's eat.'"

As everyone dug in, I sent a witch-whisper to Samuel's ear. "Thanks for making sure I get the grandmother-third-degree after dinner."

He looked guiltily at my dad's mom—who was sitting next to him—but as soon as he realized I'd witch-whispered instead of spoken aloud, he witch-whispered back, "I *am* glad you came to Agatha's and that we're friends."

My dad startled him by saying his name. "Samuel. Would you like more sparkling cider?"

Samuel wiped the guilty look off his face as soon as he realized that Dad didn't know we'd been using magic to talk to each other privately. "Yes, I would, thank you for asking."

"Suck-up," I witch-whispered, happy that I could torment him at will since witch-whispering didn't break the no-visible-magic rule.

He surreptitiously flicked a pea off his plate onto mine. "Just telling the truth." He was, too. What a geeky mortal-groupie.

I flicked the pea back, directly into the gravy swimming on his mashed potatoes. "Like I said, suck-up."

Samuel's dad cleared his throat from across the table, and Samuel turned his attention back to his dinner. He witch-whispered an apology, of sorts. "I don't want to make my dad worry about my manners. He hasn't been out of the lab since . . . in a really long time."

I looked at Samuel's dad. He was pale and thin, with puppy dog eyes much like the ones that Samuel liked to turn on me whenever I was annoyed with him. He hadn't recovered from Samuel's mom dying, which apparently was very unusual in a witch so young—so unusual that no one talked about it. "Sorry."

Uncle Mike diverted me from my curiosity about Samuel's mom by asking, "How do you like Agatha's, Pru?"

"It beats jail . . . a little." I knew better than to let my irritation run away with me. Uncle Mike can be very annoying, even on a witch scale. Mom says it's his Talent, something all true witches have. Except me, yet—or maybe ever. There are Air, Water, Fire, Earth, and Magic Talents. Uncle Mike is a Fire Talent. He can't read people's minds, but he can read their emotions—and pick them up. I tried to lower the irritation factor. "I made the cheerleading squad, though, so that's been fun."

Uncle Mike scoffed, "Cheerleading? Why don't you go

in for a real sport, Pru? When I was at Agatha's, I played Dragon Ball."

"Dragon Ball Z is not a sport!" That from my mortal cousin Scotty.

Mom got her "put out the fire" look and dropped her fork on her plate. "I think Uncle Mike meant football, didn't you, Uncle Mike?"

"Yeah, right. Football. Only not for sissies," he muttered. Should I mention again that Uncle Mike (short for Michelangelo—no, he's not the famous sculptor, he was just named for him) is on my mom's side of the family? Technically, he's her uncle, not mine. He and my grandfather are twins, which is rare among witches. And they're identical, which is almost unheard of. It's a little gross thinking of him going to Agatha's when he was young, about a zillion years ago.

My cousin Scotty, a senior football star at a mortal high school, could always be counted on to diss the cheer factor too. "Pru wouldn't want to break a nail or anything."

I smiled at him sweetly. "A girl's got to have good nails. I'm glad I taught you something."

Dorklock unexpectedly jumped to my defense. "Scotty, you should get her to show you how to do a backflip. She's pretty good."

Scotty laughed. "I'm more into tackling, kid."

To my surprise, my uncle Steve—who tended not to say

anything at all except yes or no because my aunt Donna would inevitably contradict him—laughed and said, "You mean you're more into *being* tackled."

Scotty scowled, and I realized, just for a second, that even football stars have their problems. I felt a little guilty about letting my own irritation turn our dinner sour, so I tried to turn it around. "I could teach you a neat backflip you could use to leap over your opposition."

Everyone laughed. I would have been more annoyed at the lack of respect for my talents (lowercase) if I hadn't noticed that Mom and Dad relaxed when the subject of Dragon Ball had been safely skated past.

Of course, neither of my grandmothers had forgotten Samuel's toast. I had to clear away the dishes in between well-aimed advice on my (nonexistent) love life.

Grandma Edna (Dad's mom): "He's a very serious young man, Pru, and so polite. He reminds me of your father at that age. But remember, you want to get your career going strong before you settle down."

Grandmama (Mom's mom): "He's a nice enough boy, I suppose. But the family—I don't like to lay the parents' sins at the feet of the child." She looked at Grandma Edna, and then back at me. Her eyebrows wiggled with significance. "Still, you don't have time for distractions. You have to concentrate on school and on"—with a look at Grandma Edna—"finding your Talent."

I put down the platter with the turkey carcass and took a deep breath before I said as authoritatively as I could, "We're just friends."

I rarely saw my grandmothers have the same reaction to anything at the same time. But they both looked at me like my words had gone through some grandmother-interpreting-machine and come out as, "I'm deeply obsessed and am planning to run away and ruin my life."

Before they could say anything, I held up the wishbone I'd fished from the turkey and waved it around to empha-size my point. "What is it with everyone? No one used to doubt a word I said." I looked at Mom first, Dad second. They had both done this to me. "Now that we live in Salem, it seems like I can't do anything right. According to you, I can't even know that my friend is just a friend and not a bad romance waiting to happen."

Dad came to my rescue. "Don't worry about Pru. She has her priorities straight. She's been studying so hard, and at the same time she's helped her cheerleading team do a fund-raiser and start competing, like she did with her old team."

Okay. It was only a partial rescue. They were my grand-mothers, after all. It was their job to put me under the microscope and torment me on the holidays. Tradition and all that.

Grandma Edna: "I'm so proud of you, but you're look-ing a bit tired. Are you getting enough sleep?"

Grandmama: "Sleep? There's time enough for sleep when she's old like we are, Edna. But competition with"—another glance at Grandma Edna—"other schools? Is that a wise idea?"

"I'm fine." I hugged Grandma Edna. "I'm more than fine." I hugged Grandmama. I looked at them both. "Trust me. Okay?"

They smiled and hugged me. But they clearly weren't ready to trust me. Sigh. Sure, I had a lot of challenges ahead. My regular magic classes began in a week. If my team didn't get a bid for Nationals at our second shot at Regionals two weeks after that, we were out of luck for this year. Scary thought, since we were far from competition gold in our routines yet.

But, I could do it. I *would* do it. Even if it killed me.

Before all the family togetherness did me in, I slipped off to my room. I sat in the turret window and watched the quiet Salem street in front of my house. And I wondered how I was going to survive—no, *thrive*—the rest of my junior year. I wasn't even willing to think about senior year yet.

I heard a faint sound and turned to see nothing—no, wait. There was a Thanksgiving card on my bed. It had a picture of a turkey with a big belly and a big smile. Inside, it said, "Have a great T-day, 666 girl. Wish I was there—*not*."

Daniel. He was the only one who called me 666 Girl. I waited for the card to smoke up and disappear, like all the other notes he had sent me over the last months had done.

But this time the card stayed in my hand. I tucked it into a drawer. Daniel was a distraction I didn't need. He'd been a bad boy from the first time he'd sent erasers flying toward my face. He'd run away, and I didn't have any time to puzzle out why he kept tormenting me with these random notes. I had a social ladder to climb.

I had to do something about the serious lack of respect I was getting. I was the girl who'd had Beverly Hills High School wrapped around my little finger. Everyone listened to me. Here? It was like my voice was the whistling wind.

Okay. It may only be the end of November, but I, Prudence Stewart, am making my New Year's resolutions early. It's crunch time, and I don't have any more squirm room. Like Yoda says, it's "Do or not do. There is no try."

First resolution: Stop wishing I wasn't a witch. Cold turkey on that one.

Not that I haven't been trying to buy into the being-a-witch-is-great idea since my parents moved us here just in time for me to begin my junior year of high school.

No. It's the mortal-life-is-over part I'm having trouble with. I know I'm a witch. I may not have manifested that darned Talent that all the other witches have manifested by my age. But I will. I know it just the same way I knew I would get boobs eventually. And I did (the real kind too, not silicone like some of my more impatient former classmates).

But I'm having trouble doing the "just say no" thing to

practically everything I've ever known and done my whole mortal life. Solution? A new, uber-self-disciplined Pru.

I had to study 24/7 to pass my classes before? Fine. I'll make it 48/14 for my new schedule of regular magic classes. No problem.

Agatha, the headmistress of the school, hates me because my mortal ways are disruptive? And maybe a little because her great-great-great-great-grandson Daniel ran away right after kissing me? Okay. I'll show her I'm the best little witch in the world. No more problems from the Pru-ster.

My cheerleading team doesn't get what it takes to win a national competition? Fine. I'll make them listen if I have to use a hair straightener as a weapon . . . or an incentive.

Boys? My luck is bound to change on that score. It was just bad luck that the first boy I had a crush on in my new school ran away. And even worse luck that the second, my hottie neighbor Angelo, is sadly off-limits because he's a mortal. Third time's the crush-charm. Or I'm meant to be happy alone. Whatever. I can't think about that right now.

My mom is going to be the new librarian at my school? Hmm. I'll have to brainstorm that one. Maybe I just won't ever go to the library. Yeah. That should work.

So I have a few obstacles to winning the Nationals, mastering magic, and finding my true Talent and a date for prom. But I can handle it. All I need is to make a list, make a plan, and trust myself, even if no one else will.

Chapter 2

I was nervous enough on Monday morning—
I had a new-and-improved plan to implement, after all—so
it didn't really help when I came down for breakfast and
found Mom in the kitchen, dressed for work, with her
purse, a battered, beat-up old thing that only a bag lady
would love, over her shoulder.

I sighed and felt my stomach slump to my toes. "I guess
you weren't kidding about the job thing?"

Dorklock looked up from his pancakes and examined
Mom's wardrobe as if he was just noticing that she was a
little dressed up for breakfast with the fam. "Is today your
first day at Pru's school?"

"It is." Mom smiled at me absently as she whirled the

breakfast dishes away, including my cereal bowl and cereal.

I saved my bowl from the whirlwind of dishes and summoned it to me. "Why couldn't you get a job at Tobias's school? Or at McDonald's? Anywhere but Agatha's."

"I know, honey. But you'll survive." Mom seemed sure of it.

"Let's hope." I gave up. There was no hope of changing her mind. And who knows what Agatha would do if her new interim librarian didn't show up?

"I was wondering," Dorklock said. "Can you check out some of the high school books for me? They won't let me have them at my school."

"What books?" Mom knew him well enough to be suspicious of the Dorklock asking about anything that wasn't video game–related.

"*Metaphysics for the New Millennium*." He looked so innocent, I knew he had to be up to something. But I was too busy trying to figure out how to do well in school when I couldn't go to the library for the foreseeable future to waste time worrying about it.

Mom didn't seem to know what the scam was either. She patted her hair, as if she cared what she looked like, and said, "I'll see. I haven't heard of that one."

"It's new." Tobias looked so angelically innocent that I knew the book must have something in it that Mom was going to hate, especially as the new high school librarian.

My mom was going to be a librarian. Interim. I wonder what that meant about the regular librarian. I sent my untouched cereal bowl spinning to the sink. I was no longer hungry. "What happened to Mr. Munjoy?"

"Nothing. He just heard about this very interesting artifact on Atlantis, and he's taken a sabbatical to go study it."

Atlantis? That sounded fishy to me, pardon the pun. "I thought Atlantis wasn't real."

Mom looked at me and sighed. "Sometimes I wonder if Agatha is right, and I have neglected your education. Atlantis is perfectly real, and I'll make sure to plan a vacation there this summer so you and Tobias will both understand how important it is to our history." She opened her hand and summoned a small mirror to check that her makeup was okay.

"Great." I think my sarcasm meter was dialed up pretty high by the stress of knowing everything I had to accomplish in the next few weeks, because it got through to Mom.

She looked up from the mirror just long enough to give me a halfhearted smile. "Don't worry. I promise to treat you just as I would any other student if I see you in the library."

"Don't *you* worry," I shot back. "I don't go to the library." And I wouldn't either, as long as my mom was there. Gah!

The rest of the day matched my morning. Sure, the hallway with the lockers was exactly the same. But the first day of real magic classes made me question why I'd been so sure it was a good idea to test out of remedial—against the advice of Agatha and Mr. Phogg (aka Skeletor and/or Skin and Bones). Remedial classes are small. Regular classes are . . . not.

Because I'd changed my class schedule, I had math first. I still had my hottie math teacher—but my crush on him had been seriously cooled off by the 411 that he'd been at school with Mom. Talk about TMI. But I'm over it now. Math was a subject that translated well from the mortal realm to the witch realm, so Mr. Bindlebrot's class didn't figure large into my new plan of attack—as long as I didn't have to shortchange studying for math tests because I was studying for my magic classes.

Which, I realized about ninety minutes into my first day out of remedial classes, was a total possibility. My first "real" magic class was transubstantiation. In remedial class, I'd become an expert at the whole rabbit-out-of-the-hat thing— although sometimes the rabbit was blue, or maybe a gerbil. And once, the hat was a baseball cap.

Not that any of that small stuff I sweated meant a thing today. Mr. Phogg looked a little more alive in a classroom of motivated students. He smiled at us in a creepy teaching-dead kind of way. I actually had some small hope of liking this class, until he pointed toward a big jar filled with clear liquid and dead frogs. "Today, you will dissect a frog." He materialized data sheets in front of each of us. "Record every organ, muscle, and bone, please." Then he clapped his hands. "You have one hour. Begin now."

Everyone else hopped to, forgive the bad pun. I took a moment to shake away the paralysis that comes with knowing that I was, once again, clueless. I'd done the whole dissection thing last year in Beverly Hills, so I wasn't as freaked out as I might have been. Mainly, I was puzzled. What did transubstantiation have to do with dissection? Was I going to have to take chemistry all over again? I thought my credits from Beverly Hills should have transferred, but since Headmistress Agatha hated my guts, I could be wrong.

But then, as frogs began to float toward our lab tables, it became horribly clear to me: We were supposed to dissect our frogs with magic. The tiny little organs, muscles, and bones were supposed to be removed one by one without benefit of a scalpel or minute forceps.

Oh, goody. This is what I get for testing out of remedial magic classes: a chance to fail spectacularly in front of my classmates.

Somehow, I managed to get that frog apart—and back together, too. I'm not sure how I did it, though, and I'm really hoping no one ever asks me to do it again.

The rest of the day was full of equally fun revelations about the rigors of regular magic classes. For one thing, I suddenly was seeing a lot more of Mr. Phogg than I was used to. He was teaching the potions class, too. The odd thing was that even though seeing him reminded me of my torturous sojourn in remedial classes, he was starting to grow on me. In a noncreepy way. In front of students who were able and motivated to learn, he wasn't quite as grumpy or mean. I realized, despite the fact he looks like a walking skeleton, he knew his magic.

Lunch was the one time of day that was absolutely normal. Pretending to be oblivious to the frowns of my fellow cheerleaders, who were waiting for me at "our" table, I stopped by the fringie table to say a quick hi to Samuel, Maria, and Denise. They were the ones who'd let me join them on the first day of school, when no one else could be bothered. It didn't matter to me that I got ribbed for talking to them once I got to the cheerleaders' table. I had no intention of wiping the snipe bull's-eye off my back by hurting the three people who'd been my only friends in those first horrible days at my new school, when I thought I might sink to the bottom of the social pool and drown in invisibility.

Samuel, as usual, popped a chair for me. Even though he's a mega-genius and I've explained (at least once a week) the whole bonding-by-meal process necessary for good team dynamics, he likes to pretend I'm going to sit with them.

I looked at the chair, then at him grinning at me. "Very funny." I popped the chair away.

"How are you doing?" Maria was the kind one. "Are the regular classes much harder for you?"

"Not too bad," I lied. "I haven't made a fool of myself yet."

Denise laughed. "That's what you think. The look on your face when the frogs came floating at you? I don't think I was the only one who noticed." Note, Denise is not the tactful one of my three fringie friends.

"Hey!" I raised my eyebrows, hoping she'd understand the universal girl sign for "back off." "I got the dissection done, didn't I?"

"Sure, you did." She grinned so wide, the freckles on her cheeks were really noticeable.

I didn't like her smirk. "What do you mean?"

She stopped smirking and looked a little surprised. "Didn't you notice a few of those itty-bitties lifted themselves out for you?"

"*You* helped me?" I wasn't going to admit I hadn't noticed the magical helping hand.

Maria patted Denise on the shoulder. "That was nice of you." Yeah. Especially since we all knew Denise was not the nice one.

Denise glanced at Maria. "First day. It's not going to be a habit."

Samuel flipped his funny tri-lens glasses at me. "Don't worry, Pru. You'll catch up. It's not that hard once you get the hang of it." This would have been more reassuring if he hadn't already aced chemistry a year early and hadn't been enrolled in senior metallurgy this year. Like I said, he's on the mega-wattage side of brilliant.

"I know what I have to do—the problem is the mega-to-do list I've got going on. Back in Beverly Hills, I'd have used the PDA function on my cell. What do kids in Salem use to keep track of the impossibly huge list of things to do to keep from getting flushed down the grade drain?"

They all three looked at me like I was speaking gibberish. Then Samuel smiled. "I have some ideas. Let me play with them in my lab for a while, and I'll see what I can do to help you keep on track."

"And the cavalry arrives," Denise said snarkily.

Maria giggled. "The geek cavalry, at least."

"We cheerleaders don't know how to do geek." I sighed. "Gotta go join my squad. I see the laser eyes of disapproval being aimed at me. Later."

Like fringies everywhere, they shrugged off the idea that I could get in trouble with my fellow cheerleaders for talking to them. That's what I liked about them. That, and that after I talked to them, I felt better about getting the hang of regular magic class. Samuel has come through for me before. I knew I could trust him when he said he'd find a solution for me.

Geeks can be a girl's best friend, you know. Even if the girl in question is a cheerleader who only half understands geeks herself.

✳

Tara, the head cheerleader, didn't look my way when I finally sat down at our lunch table. I was so tired from trying to keep up in class, that I just sat and ate and let everyone talk around me. I knew I'd have to think of a way to appease her by practice time, but I didn't have the energy for it without a nice, satisfying peanut butter and guava jelly sandwich.

Unfortunately, no brilliant ideas light-bulbed their way into my brain while I was busy in my new precognition class. I thought I'd followed the teacher—a rather rotund, Santa Claus–like figure with a bushy white beard—pretty well. Until he assigned our homework: use the family scrying crystal to check our final grade at the end of the class.

The good news was that we would then be able to adjust our work to improve our grades, or so he said. The bad news, which I didn't need a scrying crystal to foresee: My grade was not going to be very high. After all, I hadn't even realized my family had a scrying crystal. Sigh. Why does my mother forget to tell me these things?

I thought about going to the library and asking her. But the idea of anyone else finding out my mom was school librarian cooled my annoyance off quickly. I could wait until I got home. After all, I'd have to ask her where the crystal was. I'd certainly never seen it in the potions cupboard—the one she also forgot to tell me about—all the times I'd been in there.

Instead, I stumbled into practice feeling like the letter L was glowing on my forehead like a scar worthy of Harry Potter. Not the best mind-set for getting a head start on my early New Year's resolutions. But, a witch has got to do what a witch has got to do.

My second early New Year's resolution is to make friends—or at least firm allies—with Tara. Head cheerleaders, whether witch or mortal, are the gatekeepers to every cheerleader's reputation. If the head cheerleader says you're golden, you glow. If she says you're mud, you ooze as far away as possible. So far, Tara had only been willing to grant me gold-plate status—in exchange for several favors in return, of course. Unfortunately, in her eyes, my friendship with the fringies kept tarnishing my shine.

Girl drama. Even I don't understand it all the time. But Tara hadn't talked to me at lunch, and it wasn't an oversight.

I sneaked a peek at her in the locker room as she went over her plans for practice with her second-in-command, Charity. I couldn't help remembering that position had been mine on my old mortal team back in Beverly Hills. Not only had I been second-in-command my sophomore year, but I would have been head cheerleader this year if we hadn't moved to Salem. I'm getting used to the fact that my life has changed permanently. There are even a lot of pluses to being able to do magic. But sometimes it stings like a BOTOX needle stuck in too deep and twisted too hard.

I took a few deep breaths to get the oxygen going. I had a goal, I couldn't waste time. I had to get on Tara's good side again. The question was, where to start? Tara hadn't liked me when I first came to Agatha's Day School for Witches (first understatement—she'd thought I had mortal cooties). She hadn't thought I should be on the team (second understatement—she'd thought I couldn't possibly know anything useful for cheerleading witches).

I've managed to get our relationship to one of mutually assured scowling, but it needed to go up a few notches to outright kiss-kiss-on-the-cheek-cheek before I could be sure the cold shoulder I got at lunch today wouldn't turn into a frozen shove off the team.

After two months, though, I was beginning to wonder if she was ever going to recognize how much improvement I'd brought to the team. Some of the other cheerleaders got it, I think. At least, they listened to me when Coach Gertie told them to do what I said. The Salem Witches had been super sloppy before I came along. Sure, they could fly and dip and twirl in the air. But their V's looked like U's, and their coordination was . . . uncoordinated, to say the least.

I'd almost gained some of the respect I'd lost moving from one school to another when I showed them how to compete at the regional competition (for mortals, but still . . .). Losing had put a dent in my progress, despite the fact that I'd opened the eyes of the whole team to the fact that I actually knew what I was talking about when it came to what was necessary for winning. R-E-S-P-E-C-T. That's what I mean. That's what I need. Oh, and to manifest that frappilicious Talent that everyone else, even timid little Celestina, had already manifested.

I stopped hesitating. There was really no way to be sure Tara wouldn't suddenly sabotage my efforts to get fifteen cheerleading witches to work together as a team and forget about grandstanding during competition.

Sigh. Resolutions always look so much more doable when they're neatly bullet-pointed.

I didn't have time to waste. It was only going to take one step. Just one huge squeeze of my heart. Call it a blood sacrifice. Tara was interested in my mortal neighbor, Angelo. So was I, even though I'd sworn off everything mortal (except talking to my dad . . . and cheering, of course). I'd tried other ways to make the cheer bond tight with Tara. Tried to show her I was solid gold, not gold-plate. Maybe even second-in-command-worthy. But I was still dangling on the edge of being rubber-stamped "tarnished" and put on the sidelines.

I'd tried everything else I could think of. It was time for the blood sacrifice. I'd have to be true to the Dorklock's favorite movie star, Yoda. No more "try" and "maybe." I knew the one way to get Tara on my side: become her pipeline to time with Angelo. In other words, stand back and give her permission to poach my crush.

"Hey, Tara." I kept it casual, pretending not to notice that she hadn't looked my way when I called her name. "Angelo's coming over on Saturday. He was hoping you might drop by, and I said I'd ask to see if you were free." This, of course, was an out-and-out lie. Angelo *was* coming over Saturday—to put wooden tents over our bushes to protect them from the winter snow that was due any day. He just hadn't asked about Tara.

She struggled, and Charity tried to help by putting her hand on her arm and physically encouraging her to resist the temptation. But Angelo, though mortal, was not someone Tara wanted to write off her list just because she was mad at me.

She shook off Charity's hand and turned, equally casual, as if everyone in the locker room didn't know she'd been freezing me out a nanosecond ago. "I thought you swore off mortal things for a while? You know, to make Agatha happy?"

Sure, bring up Agatha. "Whatever. Angelo's coming over because I can't be totally impolite and shake my neighbors. I'm not into him or anything." Lie. Not that she'll pick up on it. She's too busy thinking about Angelo for herself. "But if you have more important plans . . ." Yes. Not only can I stick the knife in, I can twist it real good.

"I don't have more important plans, but shouldn't you?" Tara could twist the knife too.

"What do you mean?" I'd expected a little more enthusiasm from her. I was beginning to think even Angelo wasn't enough to turn Tara to the Pru side.

"You know, manifesting your Talent, studying so you can learn enough magic to pass your classes? That's going to be hard with Angelo around, isn't it?"

"Yes." Ouch. Clearly, I hadn't phrased the invite in a way that put me in her debt. Tara didn't want to owe me one? Okay. That was easy to fix. "So? You caught me. I'm really hoping you can keep him occupied while I'm busy studying. He's totally cramping my magic-cramming-session style."

Bingo. Now that *she* was doing *me* a favor, she had a big smile. "I wouldn't want you to fail your classes and get suspended from the team." Tara earned a frown from Charity for this little pink lie. "After all, we have Regionals coming up in two weeks. And we all"—she casually waved toward the girls crowding around to enjoy the drama—"know how much it means to you to get an invite to Nationals and get the chance to beat your old team." Her whole attitude said, "Snap! Got you good, you mortal-hugger."

"Good to know you've got my back," I said, not letting myself wonder how many ways I'd hate it if she and Angelo hit it off. Of course, it was not against Yoda's teaching for me to hope that Angelo and Tara made the world's most awful couple. "You'll keep Angelo distracted, and I'll be able to sneak some study time in while he's over."

"Perfect." Tara looked happy. Charity did not.

I figured I should go for what I really wanted most from Tara while the whole deal with Angelo was still smoking hot. "I had an idea about practices, to get us ready for the finals."

"It's not your job to have ideas." Charity frowned at me. "It's Tara's. She has the Inspiration Air Talent, after all." I couldn't blame her for sticking up for Tara—it was her job. In fact, I'd kind of counted on it.

"I know. It's just that I have been on a winning team. I know what it takes. I just thought I'd throw out some ideas. Tara will decide which ones will work with our team, of course." I smiled at her, but her frown turned into a scowl. Maybe she read my thoughts: I can be obsequious to the max when the national championship is on the line.

Tara wasn't buying the obsequious bit either. Her frown was much daintier than Charity's. She even threw in a sigh that demonstrated her uber-patience with the slow girl. "I hope you're not going to suggest we practice like mortals again."

"Why not? We don't have a lot of time. It'll be fun!" I tried to put some cheer-enthusiasm into "fun" in the hopes I could carry them with me. They all stared at me as if I'd tried to convince them that cleaning the locker room with their tongues would be a blast.

Sometimes I wished I could have snapped my fingers and reconstructed my rep from my old school. There, it had been gospel according to Pru when it came to cheering. And fashion. And boys. Sigh.

Everyone looked at Tara. She tapped her fingers together for a bit while she thought it over. For exactly six seconds—I counted. "Maybe. But first we should go spy on your old team—just you and me—and see what they're up to."

Charity didn't like the "just you and me" bit. "We've already seen them. They're not going to be doing anything we didn't see on our field trip."

I agreed with Charity. Besides, checking out my ex-best-friend and crush-poacher Maddie and the other cheerleaders at Beverly Hills High was not on my list of new resolutions. We'd taken a school-sanctioned field trip—invisibility bubble and all—with the whole squad a few weeks ago. I didn't see any point to reliving that torture.

Except, of course, that Tara already knew that. She was standing there, waiting for me to refuse. Weeyotch.

If she thought I was going to waste my blood sacrifice by refusing to squirm a little at the sight of Maddie with my old crush Brent, she didn't have a clue about how committed Prudence Stewart was to taking the Salem Witches to the top of the national championship. "If that will convince you, we can go."

"Great." Tara's expression almost matched her voice—she

was head cheerleader, after all. "That will help me decide whether we should follow your suggestion and practice like mortals." She looked at me. "Or if we should even bother with mortal competition."

I didn't let myself react. She was trying to get to me, and I wasn't going to let her. Besides, two could play that "pass the hot potato" game. "Fine. But why waste time watching them practice? Better to watch them compete." She needed to understand the difference between great cheering and merely good cheering if I expected her help in getting the girls in shape for the next regional competition. We needed to place in a regional to get an invite to Nationals.

"Even better." She didn't see the trap coming. She thought she'd trumped me good, and still gotten face-time with Angelo.

"Great. See you Saturday."

Her eyes narrowed as she realized the trap. She couldn't spend Saturday with Angelo if she was watching my old team compete. "But—"

"Angelo will wait. The team comes first, right?" I couldn't help it if my smile was just a little too happy.

With the team watching her, Tara was stuck. "Fine."

Of course, so was I. Stuck going to see my old best friend with my old crush. Stuck watching my old team—the one I would have been head cheerleader of. The one I would be leading to the national championship if I hadn't moved to

Salem. Was it petty of me to hope they didn't win while I was in the stands watching? Probably. But it is what it is.

"Maybe you can reschedule Angelo for Sunday?" Tara asked. Well, really, ordered, though it did sound like a question. "Saturday at the competition and Sunday with Angelo work for me. That way, we won't have to counter any protective spells from Agatha's. It'll be a snap to get around our parents' spells on the weekend."

She had a good point. The headmistress of my new school hated me enough already. I so didn't need her to catch me breaking school rules. Again.

Chapter 3

Samuel came over after practice for our regularly scheduled tutoring session. He caught me slumped over the newly discovered family scrying crystal. I'd been trying to find out what the future held for my old team at the regional competition this weekend, but all I'd managed to do was get a teensy blue glow that revealed . . . absolutely nothing.

My new kitten/familiar Sassy jumped from the table, where she'd been nosing the egg-sized crystal, to his shoulder and began licking his hair. Traitor. Shouldn't my familiar stick with me, even if I'm not the best witch in the room?

"How's it scrying, homey?" he asked, grinning widely and holding his hands behind his back. Instead of lifting her from his shoulder, he was trying to fend Sassy's ticklish tongue off by shaking his head. Clue #1 that he has some new invention for me.

Clue #2 came when he tossed something furry in my lap. Sassy rowred, leaping from his shoulder to my lap with lightning speed, and pounced on it.

"Cut it out, Sassy!" I commanded, lifting her tiny body off the furry thing. She stalked off.

"What's this?" I smoothed back the neon blue fur, which turned out to be a swath of plastic hair crowning a lumpy plastic figure. It looked like a Troll doll, which had been hot in the 70s. Samuel was certainly capable of giving me a non-hot gift. But a Troll doll? Was it some kind of secret message that only another fringie would understand?

He flipped his glasses at me, obviously disappointed that I wasn't more enthralled by his gift—and definitely shocked that I didn't instantly know what it was that he'd created for me. "*It* is To-Do the Troll."

Cute. It had a name only a mother could love. "To-Do?" Of course: I'd said I needed a witch version of a PDA, so naturally Samuel instantly thought Troll doll. Geeks. Sigh.

He blinked at me, apparently thrown by my lack of enthusiasm for all things Troll. "To keep track of all your tests, dates, papers, practices—you know," he explained. "Like a to-do list, only bossier."

"Bossier?" I looked at the Troll doll again. Sure, it looked grumpy and mean. But bossy? Was it going to whip me with its long blue hair?

Samuel grinned and crossed his arms, watching me for a minute, as if he thought I'd figure it out. Finally, he sighed and uncrossed his arms. "Tap it."

"Tap it?" It seemed like a harmless request—to someone who didn't know that Samuel invented things like incredible tingling bracelets and rings that buzzed when you acted like a mortal. Of course, those things had come in handy in my first few months at Agatha's, when I wasn't sure I could cut it as a student—or a witch.

He sighed again, a long, gusty, fringie-frustration sigh. "Tap it, Pru." Samuel was generally patient. But much less so when he had a new invention to show off.

I tapped the Troll doll gingerly and hastily withdrew my finger in case it began to smoke or spark.

The doll, balanced on my thigh, bent over at the waist and then straightened up sharply, flipping its long blue hair to the back. It smoothed down the hair with pudgy Troll fingers as it looked at me. "Hello, Prudence. What may I add to the list for you today?" The voice was cultured, a deep baritone that couldn't have been more wrong for the grumpy-looking doll.

I looked at Samuel. "You decided to give a Troll doll the voice of an English butler?"

"Makes a nice contrast, doesn't it?" He smiled and didn't

offer to change the voice for me. Very un-Samuel of him. "So tell him your list."

The doll—To-Do—waited patiently, blinking his big eyes at me and running his hands down his hair as if to tame the thready blue mess. Waste of time, but what else did he have to do?

You know what they say about doing Roman stuff when you're in Rome? When it comes to fringie geeks, it's exactly the same. I stopped fighting the inevitable. Samuel's gizmos usually came with a twist, but they worked for me. "My list? How about 'win Nationals'?"

Samuel said, "Say, 'Win National Cheerleading Championship.'"

I repeated dutifully, "Win National Cheerleading Championship."

To-Do blinked and repeated, "Item #1: Win National Cheerleading Championship. Priority level?"

Priority level? "Critical."

To-Do growled and blinked. "I beg your pardon?"

Samuel whispered, "It will be high, medium, or low."

I looked at him, still not totally getting this new invention he'd given me. "That's unimaginative of you." Okay, so I was being unfair to someone who had made me a talking butler to keep track of my to-do list. But he'd made him look like a Troll doll!

"May I have the priority level of Item #1 again, please?"

"Pretty darn high, I'd say." I thought about how hard it had been to sacrifice Angelo to Tara. I wouldn't do that for any medium-level priority, I was sure of that.

"I beg your pardon?"

Samuel sighed. "Just say high. Nothing else. Okay? I didn't have time to make him understand generalizations."

"Well, okay then." I rolled my eyes at the doll standing there waiting for me to speak. "High."

"Thank you. Item #1. Win National Cheerleading Championship. High priority. Action Step #1, please?"

I looked at Samuel. He said, "What's the first step toward winning Nationals?"

Duh. The Troll was really throwing me off my game. "Practice like mortals."

After I'd outlined seven action steps to winning Nationals (practice like mortals, write a killer routine, fund-raise the application fee, get Coach Gertie to send in the forms, create team unity, get entire team focused on winning, perform a killerly perfect routine to wow the judges), I really got into the swing of the ugliest talking to-do list ever.

Then we moved on to Item #2: maintain passing grades so I could be on the cheering team. The action steps for this one were fewer: study, tutoring sessions with Samuel, scrounge for as much extra credit and bonus points for class participation as I could.

I'd debated the extra-credit and class participation action step, but I couldn't see any way around it. Being the kind of kid who raises her hand first and goes to the teacher to get more work was going to cost me kewl points, for sure. But everything hinged on passing all my classes, because otherwise, I'd be off the team. And then my to-do list would be an I'm-screwed list.

Compared to the first two items, the rest of my list looked easy-peasy: figure out how to manifest my Talent, clean my room, set the table for dinner every night, don't fight with Dorklock. Keeping on my mom and dad's good sides suddenly seemed very important. I needed them to think I was Wonder-Daughter, just in case I suddenly required a major parental intervention to save my school career.

There wasn't a lot of time left for our regular tutoring session, but Samuel did manage to show me how to get the cloudy blue glow of my scrying crystal to reveal a dim scene from the future. At least, I thought it was a view of my future. Not that I could tell what the blob I thought was me was doing.

As I got ready for practice the next day, To-Do very helpfully reminded me of Action Step #1 to winning Nationals: practice like mortals. I thought about waiting until after Saturday, but there was so little time—two weeks—before our next regional competition that I decided to push my luck with Tara all the way to the brink.

I tried approaching her before practice, out of earshot of the other girls, so I could have her on my side before I brought the subject up to Coach Gertie and the other girls. "If we really want to win this, I need you to help me convince Coach Gertie to bind our powers during practice."

Unfortunately, Tara was not quiet about her reply. She practically shouted, "Bind our powers? Are you crazy? Pru, I think you're going way too far with this whole 'it's fun to practice like mortals' kick."

I raised my voice to a more normal level when I saw the other girls suddenly start paying attention to the conversation—witches can listen from a distance, if they know there's something juicy to listen to. "It isn't just that I think we can have fun cheering the mortal way, it's also the best way to get into the winning mind-set. We've only got two weeks."

Tara shook her head like she couldn't believe how dumb I was. "If we fall on our heads we're going to be in the *ouch* mind-set. What good is that?"

I didn't have a lot of ammunition to gun that one down. So I went for the lame but true motto of sportsmen and women everywhere. "No pain, no gain."

She gave me a look that said she thought I was not only Talentless, but plain crazy, too. "Only someone who thinks like a mortal could say that."

I could feel the other girls siding with her, and desperation made me fight back with all I had. "Only someone who thinks like a mortal can win a mortal cheering competition." Take that, Ms. Tara Tart-Witch.

Coach Gertie blew her whistle for us to begin practice.

"Look," I said. "How about we practice like mortals until you and I catch the competition. Then, if you still don't understand why I think it's necessary, I promise never to bring it up again and we can go back to full-magic practice. Okay?"

"You're that sure of yourself?" Tara was torn. She chewed her bottom lip and looked at the other girls, who had stopped and were staring at her, knowing that right now she was all that stood between them and the possibility of pain and more pain, all in the name of winning. I could see she wanted something, but I'm not even sure if she knew what it was yet.

"I want to win. I thought you did too." It was my last shot. Sure, it was low. But I was desperate.

She sighed, looked at the unhappy members of our team, and nodded. "For the win, it's worth it." She flashed me a smile. "But you really have to drop the mortal rah-rah or I'm not going to be able to keep you from social suicide much longer."

I wasn't happy to be threatened, and I guess it showed, because she smiled and said, "Guess what? I looked up the schedule and the Witches' football team will be playing

Angelo's school next. We should invite him to keep us company while we cheer."

Right. Angelo. My mortal neighbor with the hottie factor of 10 squared. My blood sacrifice. I smiled like it didn't hurt. "I'm sure he'll be happy to defect. He doesn't think his team is doing that well this year, anyway." I wondered if my competition hopes were wasted. How well can a team do if the head cheerleader doesn't care if she wins?

I summoned To-Do while everyone else headed in for practice. It took three tries before he understood that the action step "Throw Tara and Angelo together once a week" belonged under "Win National Competition." Oh, well.

As I entered the gym, I heard Coach Gertie cast a binding spell. The girls were groaning, but Tara gave me a smile. She was really enjoying making the others miserable.

I knew she was also enjoying the thought that she wouldn't have to try to fool her parents about seeing Angelo. Sneaking to see a boy is a very exciting thing to do. But sneaking when you have an accomplice is easier on the nerves.

I didn't like to think of myself as an accomplice, but as I watched the girls getting the routines down so cold, they were practically iced—fear of pain is a powerful motivator for getting things right—I wished I could scry into the future well enough to make sure that this would get us to Nationals.

Chapter 4

I told Mom that Tara and I had a school project to work on, and she didn't even raise an eyebrow. I guess her Mom-dar was on the blink. Either that or I've just gotten very good at being plausible. So far, her work as a librarian in the school was invisible to me, except that when we got back from school, we both seemed a little tired. I went right to studying, and Mom went right to making dinner and tidying up. Neither of us seemed to have much pep in our step, though.

The best thing about her new job was that Mom didn't ask nearly as many questions about how my day had been. She didn't ask Dorklock, either. Not even when he started bringing a new friend along to the house to play video games. In the past, she'd have been all over him making a new friend. Now? She just zapped them some cookies and milk and said, "Have fun, guys."

When Tara got to our house, I brought her up to my room and then we popped right to Beverly Hills. Her magic, not mine, because I was still a little bit shaky on getting places where I hadn't been before. All Tara needed was to check out a map, figure out the coordinates, and zap, there we were.

As soon as we arrived in the gym and I heard the all-too-familiar sounds of competition, I wanted to go home again. It's not like me to be a quitter, but we hadn't improved as much as I'd hoped during our week of practicing like mortals. Here, watching fantastic teams, with the team I'd known forever before the move to Salem, I wished I'd stalled Tara.

My stomach did a perfect dive roll to my toes. Every team we watched today was going to be better than we were. "Don't let the skill in this room get to you. We *can* be this good, with practice." I didn't actually think my words would change what Tara was going to experience as we sat in the stands and watched the performances. But I had to say it, like stage actors are compelled to say, "Break a leg." Maybe if Tara understood that we had a long way to go to reach competition level, she'd realize why practicing like a mortal was so important.

"Oh, please. You make it sound so hard. As if we haven't been cheering for forever. You have to stop thinking like a

mortal. The Witches are going to clean up. Trust me."
Typical kewl girl attitude.

I didn't say anything. I used to have that attitude too,
when I belonged in Beverly Hills and was so golden, I
couldn't do anything wrong. Back when I was going to be
head cheerleader of the team I was watching as they prac-
ticed just off the competition floor. They would be up soon.
I couldn't quite bring myself to hope they'd lose. But I
couldn't hope they'd win, either. Everything felt different,
wrong—me in the stands, them on the floor about to compete for their fourth win in a row.

"They're really good. Which one's the boyfriend-stealer
again?" Her voice had a malicious edge that I'd heard too
many times growing up in the kewl girl clique.

Uh-oh. I really shouldn't have told the other girls so
much about Maddie. But it had been my sweet sixteen
sleepover, and we'd been loosened up by a rousing game of
Truth or Dare.

I didn't want anything bad to happen to Maddie. Sure,
she had been my BFF, even after I moved—or so I'd
thought, until I found out that she'd poached the guy I was
interested in. Still, she hadn't meant to hurt me. Maybe.

"That one." I pointed Maddie out. She stood holding the
foot of Chezzie, the head cheerleader who'd taken my
place. Chezzie looked like a statue, poised and balance. She
didn't shake, not even a little.

Tara looked at Maddie, squinting, since we were halfway up in the stands. "Funny, she doesn't look like a backstabber."

"They never do." From the way she was holding Chezzie's foot steady, you'd never know that Maddie had once spiked Chezzie's diet soda with purple food dye so that Chezzie had a very berry smile for a solid week. She'd gone through six cases of tooth bleach to get rid of it. Not that anyone ever knew it was Maddie who'd done it, except me. As far as I know, Chezzie still thought the soda-dyer was an old boyfriend she'd just broken up with. A rumor started by me to throw people off Maddie's scent.

"No, they never do, do they? Maybe there's a spell we could cast so that backstabbers would show their true colors before we made the mistake of trusting them." She looked at me so innocently, I knew she was thinking that would be a useful spell for her to have right now. Looking back at her faux innocent smile, I had to agree.

"Shhh, they're starting. Pay attention."

From high up in the stands, among the family and friends of those competing, I watched intently, following my old squad's every move with a sense of déjà vu that made me lightheaded and giddy. I knew that routine like the back of my hand. I'd created that routine. All I wanted was to be there, on the floor with them. But that wasn't going to happen.

"They're good. But these seats aren't very comfortable." Tara was restless as the team competed.

"Here." I reached into the black backpack I'd brought with me and materialized a seat cushion for her.

"Thanks." She sat on it. "Much better." She turned her attention back to the competition at last.

I thought about explaining what my old team was doing that was so good, but decided against it. If she couldn't see it for herself, then I was wasting time trying to make her my ally.

I must have held my breath the entire time I watched, because when the final routine was over, I gasped in a breath and fought back tears.

"Do you think they nailed it?"

"Oh, yeah. None of the other teams even touched them."

I sat there, watching my old team take their bows, huge smiles on their faces. I'd been there, done that. Man, I wanted to do it again.

Tara had a little bit more bravado than usual in her voice when she said, "We can do that at Nationals."

Yeah. The Salem Witches could do that. With about two hundred synchronicity and grace spells and . . . "With a little magic, maybe."

As soon as the words were out of my mouth, I looked around nervously, realizing that I'd become careless in my few months at Agatha's. We were surrounded by mortals, after all. I'd never have been so loose-lipped when I lived among mortals every day.

"Chill, pill," Tara said, recognizing my reaction for what it was: the mortal-startle alert. Then she witch-whispered to me, "It's not like mortals don't use the word 'magic'—they just don't get that it's real."

It was like her voice was right next to my ear, even though her head was turned to watch the judges shake hands with my old squad. Here, in the stands, surrounded by mortals, it freaked me out, for some reason. But I hid my reaction this time. Her words were true enough. When I'd lived in the mortal world, I hadn't worried so much about letting my witchy roots show. But I hadn't had such starkly visible roots back then either. I hadn't been allowed to do magic, for the most part. It was rude to do magic, my mother said. Another instance of when in Rome—an all-mortal-all-the-time Rome.

"We *can* do that," I repeated, wanting to get back to my point.

"Okay. So we can." Tara looked at her arm, where a big purple bruise from practice still showed. "Why?"

"What?" I didn't understand that question at all. Wasn't it obvious? Winning was for . . . winners.

She looked at me like I was the one who was failing the competitive spirit test. "Who cares?"

Ummm. I did. And I wasn't going to let her sneak out of our agreement on the technicality that winning against mortals didn't matter. "I thought we agreed: You get some face-time with Angelo, and I get your support to make the team National-worthy."

"Cooperation is one thing, but it sounds like you want me to care."

"Of course I want you to care. Winners care."

Tara shrugged. "Competition is so . . . normal." She grinned. I knew she had drawn out the delay before "normal" just to make me worry that she was going to say "mortal." Weeyotch.

"I know you want this, and so does Coach Gertie, but I don't have to get it for real to fake it at practice, do I?"

"You're head cheerleader." I thought that said it all, but when she stared at me blankly, I added, "The other girls will know."

"They'll do what I tell them. And I'll tell them to do what you say. You'll have my support. Isn't that good enough?"

It should have been. Except that everyone on a winning team has to want it. Has to be able to taste the win and spit out the doubt. If Tara wasn't feeling it, maybe I should just give up—spend my time studying so I didn't flunk my way back into remedial classes.

"Man poacher alert." Tara gave me just enough warning that I put a smile on my face a micro-mini-second before Maddie suddenly showed up next to me in the stands. "Pru?"

"Hi, Maddie. Congratulations on the perfect routine. I

bet you have the win in the bag." I really have to hand it to myself, I sounded sincere, even when I turned and saw that Maddie was holding hands with Brent.

"Liar," Tara witch-whispered in my ear.

I ignored her and kept my focus on Maddie and Brent. "Hey, I heard through the grapevine that you two got together. I'm happy for you." I wasn't, of course. But I wasn't exactly upset, either. I looked at Brent and wondered why I'd had a crush on him. He was a bit of a follower, by the way he was trailing after Maddie like a little puppy dog.

"I've been meaning to call, but I've been *so* busy." Maddie squeezed Brent's hand and gave him a quick, adoring look. But her attention was for me—and it was unnerving that she was not showing one ounce of shame. Maddie had always been the kind of girl to blush when she hadn't done anything wrong at all. "How did you get here, Pru?"

I couldn't answer. I was still stuck on that blatant lie—she'd been "meaning to call," my Jimmy Choo–clad foot. My voice was stuck in my throat as my brain searched for something that would be kewl, cutting, and that would shred that smile right off her face—without Brent having a clue he was witnessing a verbal catfight, of course. I'd prefer he never even knew I'd planned on making him my next boyfriend if I hadn't had to move to Salem.

Tara was not so speechless. "We just popped in to check out our competition for Nationals."

Technically, true.

Maddie looked her over, assessing her correctly as the head cheerleader. There's something about the position that announces itself, even when the head cheerleader is in jeans and a cute top. "Scare you away?"

For the first time the whole day, Tara seemed focused. It took me a minute to get why. Just long enough for her to say, sweetly, "Scared? Of you? Oh, no. The Salem Witches have the secret weapon at our school now." She looked at me. Amazingly, even I would have thought she respected me if I didn't know better.

"No disrespect, but we rock." Maddie looked back to me, dismissing Tara. "Chezzie's a great head cheerleader." She put on a fake frown. "I know that was supposed to be your gig. Hope it doesn't bother you that we're doing great without you?"

"Not at all," I lied. It bothered me, all right, but not nearly as much as the change I was seeing in Maddie. What had turned her into a full-fledged beeyotch in the few months I'd been gone? "Tara's our HC. She's great, too." I didn't really think so, but I'd rather have had a Brazilian wax done one square inch at a time than admit that. Especially to this new, diamond-edged Maddie.

She didn't believe me, anyway. She flicked a glance at Tara, smiling so fake, she meant for us to know it. "Great. So I guess we'll see who's all that at Nationals, then?"

Tara smiled back, her eyes narrowing. "Well, *you* will, anyway. *We* already know."

Maddie laughed, and let go of Brent's hand to put her arm around his waist and curl her thumb in one of his belt loops. "It'll be interesting, Pru. You on one team, and me on the other."

"Yeah." I finally managed to speak. Nothing kewl or cutting. But intelligible, at least.

"See you then." Maddie walked off with Brent at her side.

For a minute I wanted to call her back, to see if the Pod People had taken her over. But then Tara distracted me by saying, "Wow. I totally get why you want the Witches to win Nationals. Are you sure you were ever BFF with that beeyotch?"

I looked at her, shocked and pleased at the sisterhood in her voice. My world was turning upside down. Tara was on my side, and Maddie was . . . the Creature from the Black Lagoon.

But we were going to take her down. Tara, me, and the rest of the team. Go, Witches!

"So. Should we have a little fun and mess up their triumph?"

"No!" Not that it wouldn't be satisfying if . . . but, no. What would Yoda say?

"I thought you put a zit spell on her not that long ago. So what's wrong with having a little fun now?" Tara's eyes were sparkly with the idea of giving my old team a little banana-peel action to mess with their competition mind-set.

I, not being clueless, knew that look should have been my signal to run. Or, technically, to fly, since we *are* witches. But that was problematic.

Problem one? We were in the bleachers, surrounded by mortals. Problem two? I half hoped Tara might convince me that it was okay to do more than psych out the team I'd hoped to lead, who were about to perform a kick-pom-pom competition routine if I didn't do something major to stop them.

It was problem three that made me say, "If we're going to beat them, we're going to do it fair and with flair." Problem three? I'm a good cheerleader, and a good cheerleader never lets jealousy, PMS, or a bad breakup cause a premature competition quake under another team's feet.

Tara looked around at the crowd of parents and friends, all focused on the championship Beverly Hills team getting ready to sweep Regionals and take it on to Nationals again. "You're such a wimp, Pru-the-mortal-lover."

I couldn't really argue with Tara. She was right. When she'd heard about Maddie, she'd been totally on my side about the zit spell. She didn't think I'd gone far enough. When I saw Maddie, the crush-poacher, macking on the guy I'd put dibs on—well, let's just say she's lucky that I'm channeling my ex-BFF rage into the performance of a lifetime at

Nationals. Oh, and also that I'm not going to let Tara go after her. Nope. It's great to have Tara on my side, but Maddie is *all* mine. I can't wait until we win. I refuse to say if. We *have* to win. I *have* to make it happen.

"Come on," Tara urged, refusing to give up. "We aren't going to hurt them. Just shake their pom-poms up a little. What's the harm in that? It's not like we're going to do anything to permanently kill their cheer mojo. Cheer mojo that comes from your notebook of routines, right?"

"True, but . . ." I stopped and looked at her and remembered her line about the backstabber-finding spell. It finally occurred to me that Tara had enough of the scoop about Maddie and me to know I'd be easy to turn to the dark side. *Too* easy. And now that I was out of remedial classes and had become Coach's Gertie's great hope to lead us to a championship, what could be more tattle-worthy than me playing unfair with mortals? Competing mortals, at that.

Definitely expel-from-school-worthy dirt, of the most exclusive nature.

But she had a point I couldn't deny: The Beverly Hills team was nothing if not great—thanks in part to me, not that they remembered that. They were lined up, smiling, completely on for the crowd and ready for the music to start.

Cheer competitions are fifty-fifty: fifty percent skill and fifty percent attitude. I knew they had the skill, and everyone could see they had the attitude. They were going to nail this routine unless the ceiling fell in, or—if Tara had her way—magic happened.

So, really, what would be the harm in creating a little spell to make them forget my routines like they'd forgotten me? No. I shook my head, refusing the temptation with every last ounce of cheer training I had. "We'll know we deserve it when we beat them at Nationals."

The music started, so loud that it beat into our bones. Tara and I watched, just like everyone else in the bleachers, as the team performed with a synchronicity and energy that made me want to be down there with them.

"They are good. Or, should I say, your routines are good," Tara commented.

"Chezzie's made some changes, but mostly they're using my routines." And they were, too. All the routines I'd created and saved up in my notebook for the time when I would be head cheerleader. My old team was performing them almost as I'd envisioned when I was writing the cheer choreography.

"Hmm." Tara actually sounded thoughtful. "You've been holding out on us. These moves are amazing." She glanced around at the mesmerized mortals around us. "Do you think you can beat your old choreography?"

Could I? "With one pom-pom tied behind my back." I wasn't going to let Tara doubt it, even if I did as I watched my routines come to competitive life.

I couldn't even be mad that they'd stolen my notebook, because I'd given it over willingly when my parents had yanked me clear across country. At the time, I'd wanted them to keep winning. But now, four months later? I wished I wouldn't get into trouble with my mom for taking the notebook back and wiping from every team member's memory that I'd ever given it to her in the first place.

Chezzie had made a few changes, of course. When you were head cheerleader, you had to put your stamp on the year, or you couldn't hold your head up high. She'd gotten rid of a solo triple backflip I'd choreographed just for Maddie. She'd replaced it with a pair of double backflips, for Chezzie and a new girl I didn't know. They were good. So good, it didn't escape me that some of the other girls watched with a little extra tension in their shoulders. Maddie was one of them. I hoped Chezzie's stellar perform-ance burned Maddie raw, deep inside her heart.

But as I watched Maddie, having lost fifteen pounds and gained the confidence to stand without wavering on the raised hands of her teammates, I knew it didn't. She was a team player, and she was busy nailing her part of the rou-tine. I remembered what that felt like, and I clapped like mad when the music and the girls stopped at exactly the same moment, routine over. Routine nailed. The crowd gave them a standing ovation.

For a teeny part of a second, I felt like a part of the team again. I felt sure that if I ran down there, magically transformed into a Beverly Hills cheerleader again, they'd pull me into the victory embrace. Credit me with helping to make the winning routine. Call me a cheer sister again.

But as I saw Maddie run off to do the victory embrace with Brent, I knew I could never go back.

The words would be right. The credit would be partially mine. But I was no longer a part of the team. They had moved past me. Way past me. If I showed up on the floor, it would be like a ghost from the past. Sure, you bow and honor her, but you don't expect her to begin eating, breathing, or living on the mortal plane again. Her time had passed. My time as a part of the Beverly Hills team had passed.

It was time to show the Witches what I could do.

Chapter 5

I stood there watching my old team, in the uniform I knew so well; I could close my eyes and feel it on me, celebrate the spectacular and no doubt winning performance as I fought the pain of knowing I was history here.

After a minute, the pain dulled enough for me to talk as if I weren't devastated by déjà vu with a sour lemon twist of never again. "I think they're going to win this competition. If they do, they'll definitely be one of the top-rated teams in the finals."

"So if we decide we want to do this national competition thing, we'll have to beat them? I know it's what you wanted. But, still, won't that be weird for you?" Tara got that glittery look again. "Facing your old team?"

"Yes." I struggled with the image of me standing with the Witches, holding the trophy, seeing the Beverly Hills team off to the side. I'd tossed the idea of competing against my old team out there once or twice in a conversation with Maddie, back when I was still talking—or rather texting—with her. But part of me never really believed that I could want to be on another team—face my old team down and win. Until now.

Now. Well, suffice it to say that all I wanted was to whip the Witches into shape, sweep the next regionals to erase our old defeat from cheer memory, and take my old team down. It would be interesting, too—the old, mortal, routine-writing me against the new, witch, routine-writing me.

I thumped back to earth. The only problem with me versus me is that both my old and new routines required a good team to carry them out. The Beverly Hills girls worked together well, understood the power of synchronicity, and didn't think muscle power was beneath them.

The Witches, well, they didn't argue that there was no I in team. But they had been quick to remind me that there *was* one in witch. The discipline and dedication—and pain—required to get us into championship form was still missing, despite my best efforts. "Can't you imagine us? Out there? The crowd clapping for us?"

"Maybe." Tara shrugged, clearly not convinced it was worth the effort. "But what if we didn't? How hard would it be for you to lose to the girl who stole your boyfriend?"

Hard. "I'd survive." Barely. Not that Maddie had really stolen my boyfriend. Technically. If I'd still been in Beverly Hills, I'm sure she wouldn't have dated Brent. Become his girlfriend. Become the Beeyotch from the planet Pod. Still, she had—despite near daily text messages between us for that first few weeks after my move—forgotten to mention that little fact to me.

"It would be sweet, though, wouldn't it?" I knew Tara was egging me on. Trying to find out how much I wanted this. "To take her down a little, like she did you?"

I saw the yellow light flashing in her eyes. It would be very dangerous to let Tara know how much I wanted this if she wasn't on board with the whole "beat Beverly Hills" motif. She'd start asking for a lot more than a little Angelo time in return. Still, I said, "Yes." Only because I knew she, of all people, wouldn't believe me if I tried to deny how much I would like to see Maddie's new ice-queen expression melt when she saw my new team beat hers.

"So would you be willing to use your"—she glanced around at the crowd, which was breaking up to go get lunch—"special skills to make sure we win?"

Before I could answer, I heard Chezzie's voice calling my name. I turned my head, going into cheering mode as my survival instincts kicked in. I plastered a rah-rah grin on my face, even though what I really wanted to do was run . . .

fly . . . away. Chezzie and I had been on the outs since grammar school. It had something to do with her seeing me do magic and my mom's mind-wipe not working perfectly. Chezzie didn't think I was a witch, though. Just the devil.

I watched as she climbed up into the bleachers. "Did you see us? I think we nailed it. What do you think?"

"I think you did too." I raised my arms in a V and pretended I had pom-poms to shake. "Go, team! Win it!"

Some of the other girls had trailed her and were climbing up into the bleachers. A nightmare in living color. No escape for the witches. Great.

There was a babble of questions that reminded me of old times. I couldn't tell who was asking what. "Did your parents let you come for a visit?" and "Weren't we great?" and "How did you get here?" I knew, however, that no one was going to allow me time to answer before the last question. When it finally came, it hurt. "Are you moving back?"

I didn't see who asked the questions, and I didn't care. I blurted out, "No way. I love Salem. Did I introduce Tara? She's the head cheerleader of my Salem team."

"So why did you come back?" There was almost a hostility to the question. Like they thought I'd come to sabotage them.

I tried to look harmless. "I wanted to see how my routines worked in competition. Mom and Dad were kewl with it. Thank goodness for the red-eye, huh? You guys were great."

Chezzie narrowed her eyes. "Yeah, we worked hard to glitter up those ideas of yours. It was great you had some notes to get us started with—really gave us a head start."

Her words swam around in my head furiously. Glitter up. Some notes. Head start. Beeyotch.

Tara had my back, surprisingly enough. "Pru's a genius with the routines, isn't she? Wait until you see what she's done for our team."

"Are you going to send us a DVD? 'Cause I don't think any of us are planning to go slumming in Salem anytime soon. Are we, girls?" There was a faint, unenthusiastic chorus of no's.

Chezzie's competition high was wearing off faster than expected. Which left her even more of a tired beeyotch than usual. So sad—for her, not me.

Tara practically purred her answer. "I meant at Nationals, of course. When we beat you."

Chezzie smiled and shook her finger at me. "It's not nice to copy other teams' routines. I'd expect you to know that, Pru. You've been on a championship team before." She looked down her plastic-surgery-perfect nose at Tara. "Unlike some people."

Big mistake. For a second, I thought Tara might turn her into a ferret, no matter what the consequences. But, instead, she just returned Chezzie's fake helpful tone. "Don't be silly. I'm not the kind of head cheerleader who'd use those routines—they're soooo last summer. Pru's been working on cutting-edge stuff for the Witches."

I might have been a bit more worried at the definition of "cutting edge" if I hadn't just then seen Maddie turn to look for Chezzie and catch sight of her talking to me. She didn't look happy to see us all standing there in the bleachers. I guess she hoped no one else on my old team would notice us in the stands. Too bad for her, Chezzie has good eyesight.

Maddie didn't start over right away. She looked at Brent first. She didn't say anything to him, just grabbed his hand and dragged him behind her as she walked slowly toward us again. Could things possibly get worse?

Chezzie looked at Tara. "Pru said you're head cheerleader?" She turned to me, and I could see her trying to decide how to dull my cutting edge. Just then, Maddie and Brent appeared. Chezzie smiled, pulling Maddie up beside her. "Guess what, Maddie! Pru's been creating cutting-edge routines for her new team. They think they're going to beat us."

"We *are* going to beat you. Without breaking a sweat." Tara wasn't afraid of making idle threats. She had the magic to back it up. Not that that would be a good thing. But I don't think she cared at the moment. I know I didn't.

Chezzie said, oh so casually, "But how can you have time for new routines when you're trying so hard to pass your classes?" She smiled at Maddie. "Isn't that what you told everyone? That Pru wasn't doing well at her new school?"

Maddie's newest betrayal sparked a slow burn inside. Sure, it was one thing to poach Brent when I wasn't around. But to tell my secrets?

The backstabber didn't even have the grace to pretend she felt shame. She just looked at me and oh-so-innocently asked, "I forgot, it's been so long ago. But didn't you say you were in remedial classes in that fancy new school of yours?"

I raised an eyebrow, thinking of how to deny Maddie's charges without outright lying. "I'm not in remedial classes. You must have misread my texts." I flicked a glance at Brent. "Maybe you were trying to do two things at once and the text message got lost in translation."

Tara had no compunction about lying. "Pru's not just a great student, she's a great cheerleader. I'm lucky to have her on my team. We're going to win Nationals this year, so start getting used to the idea of second place. 'K?"

Chezzie was done with me. She and Tara were face-to-face—and neither face was happy underneath the fake cheerleader smiles. "Have you ever competed before?"

"Don't be silly. Of course we have." Tara conveniently forgot our recent stinging loss. Easy for her, it was her first competition. Not so easy for me—I'd been on a winning team for so long, I had forgotten that there was a possibility my team wouldn't end up in the top five. "And, in one week and five hours, we'll be winning the Frozen Four Regionals."

"Is that so?" Chezzie grinned, for real this time. "Then, no offense, I think you're the one who ought to be getting used to the sound of second place—if you're lucky."

Tara raised her chin. "We're not only lucky. We're good." Good liars, anyway.

I tried not to glance at Maddie, but failed. She stared back at me like I was a stranger. And then she hooked her arm around Brent's waist. The look in her eye dared me to do something about it. Lucky for her, I didn't.

The loudspeaker announced that the judges were going to present awards and called the teams to the floor.

Chezzie gave Tara one last glare. "Whatever. Watch real winners and get a clue."

The girls moved quickly back to the floor, lining back up like the champions they were.

Tara was still fuming. Her lack of interest had undergone a transformation to an intensity that didn't bode well for Chezzie or the Beverly Hills team. "It's not too late for a little tiny earthquake, just under their feet."

"No. Don't." I knew how to use a moment, when it came my way. "We'll get them where it counts. At Nationals."

The judges called the prizes. As had become habit, the Beverly Hills team won. I stood and clapped when my old team won first place—as if it had ever been in doubt. "Cheating's not the way to win, Tara. That's not what competition is about, not even for witches."

I admit I regretted it a moment later, when Brent ran out onto the floor and folded Maddie in his arms.

Tara must have been under the mistaken impression I wasn't as steamed as she was. "So you're just going to let her get away with stealing your routines and your boyfriend?"

"She didn't steal my routines—I gave them to her." But I hadn't given her Brent. She'd definitely taken him without my blessing.

"Seems a shame you're just going to let her walk all over you." Tara was clearly unhappy with me. No doubt she would have created a spectacular failure for the team if she'd been the one feeling the way I was feeling at the moment.

I watched Maddie and Brent walk away arm in arm. I'd done this once before. I'd been invisible then, but not by choice. I'd wanted Maddie to see me, but I'd been too hurt, too scared to face what that confrontation would do to me, so I'd turned invisible without wanting to. Fear can do funny things to a person. I can attest to that first-hand.

Anger can too, apparently. Because, without even thinking hard about it, I raised my arms in the air, fixed my eyes on the departing couple, and chanted:

"Love is fine,
Love is grand.

You crossed the line,
Let your ire be fanned."

"A breakup spell?" Tara chuckled—an evil chuckle much favored by horror-movie sound guys. "I didn't think you had it in you. Good girl." Great. Tara was back to being happy now that I'd used my magic for revenge.

I thought about reversing the spell. Instead, I played the rationalization game. "It won't break them up if they don't mind fighting a lot." I smiled. I'd cast the spell knowing it wasn't a full-on breakup spell. I couldn't do that. A little trouble? Why not. Everyone knows teen love is puppy love and your first love never lasts. You could almost say I was doing them both a favor.

Tara wasn't buying my rationalization. "Yeah, well, maybe when we win it, you can deliver the final blow to that relationship without using a single whiff of magic."

"What? Run up and kiss him in front of her?" I liked the idea, but it had one flaw. "You're forgetting my crush on Brent is so last summer, know what I mean?"

"Winners don't have to want what they get, you know." She shook her head as if she were instructing a neophyte in the art of social truths.

I, however, knew exactly what she was talking about. I had been a winner. I knew what it took so much better than Tara. But she was head cheerleader, and she could make or break my transformation of the Witches. "Winning without magic is going to be tough, you know?"

Tara shrugged, her eyes following Chezzie, who was holding the trophy. She was hoisted up on her team's shoulders in triumph. "Like you say, no pain, no gain."

Chapter 6

I had done it! I had convinced Tara that winning Nationals was a goal worth winning. I would have been much happier, except I kept wondering what had made Maddie change so much in the short time I'd been gone. I mean, this was a girl who gave half of her sandwich to the smelly boy in fourth grade when he forgot his lunch.

After Tara had left my room—Mom none the wiser (maybe the new job wasn't such a bad thing after all)—my curiosity grew unbearable. It didn't take me long to realize that, as a witch, I could spy on Maddie anytime I wanted. In no time at all, I found myself in her closet—the very same closet she'd offered to hide me in when my parents yanked me out of my Beverly Hills life.

As I'd expected, the door was ajar. Maddie was always a mess, even when her parents were together and she had a maid to clean up her room every day. I'd never seen her room so messy, though. I don't think she had any clothes on hangers. Well, maybe the stuff she'd bought and then realized she hated.

I'd come alone, because I didn't know what I was going to find out. If Maddie was dissing me to everyone she knew, I'd rather some of the dirt missed Tara's ears. I didn't need two people knowing the worst of the worst about me.

Maddie was on the phone, natch. I'd always joked she'd be first in line when they made phones that could be implanted. From the way she was lying splayed across her bed, swinging her feet and giggling, I was pretty sure it was Brent on the line. Great. Just what I needed—to hear Maddie cooing with her boyfriend when I couldn't seem to find any boy interested in me as more than a friend. At least, no eligible boys, anyway.

There was only one interruption to the love-fest while I was watching. Maddie's mom came to the door with a younger man behind her. He had his hand on her back, so I guessed he was her boyfriend.

Her mom said, "We're going out for dinner, Maddie."

The boyfriend smiled and looked friendly, but I'd seen that look way too many times before on the faces of my friend's mother's new boyfriends. "We'd invite you along, but your room is much too messy. Perhaps when you are not a pig, we will take you to a nice place."

"Oink, oink," Maddie snarled back. "Who says I'd want to go to a restaurant with you, anyway?"

"Maddie, please!" Maddie's mom had that caught-between-a-rock-hard-ab-and-a-daughter look. "Armand just wants to encourage you to do better, darling."

"Right. I'll take frozen pizza and a messy room, thanks." Maddie went back to her phone call with Brent before they had even shut her door all the way. I had a feeling this scene replayed nightly at the Maddie Bedroom Theater. Her voice was so sweet and cooing with Brent, I would have thought I was dreaming the whole scene if I weren't still leaning against an old tennis racket in her admittedly piggy closet.

Unfortunately, the cooing quickly turned to snarling. Maddie practically threw her phone down after a disgusted "If you're going to be like that, I'm not going to talk to you. Good-bye."

They say revenge is a dish best served cold, and I've seen it served both hot and cold back in Beverly Hills. But what I hadn't realized before was that revenge is a dish best served in total ignorance of the taste. Because after I saw a little slice of Maddie's life—even though I was still mad at her—I knew it was much crappier than mine. Sometimes you forget that while you're struggling with the crappiola in your own life, someone else's life is handing them a pair of shoes that's one size too small and two sizes too narrow.

Maddie's mom had been happy with the role of wife and mother. She'd been unhappy when her husband walked out. And she had done one of the ten stupid things women do when they get divorced: She'd found a young, buff jerk and made herself fall blindly in love with him. Said jerk, not wanting to share the benefits of child support with the child (Maddie), was working hard to make her unwelcome in her own home.

As if that wasn't bad enough, now her mom was telling Maddie to stop trying to mess up her opportunity for true love with a real soul mate this time.

Yeah, Maddie's life was way worse than mine. Which didn't mean I didn't want to hate her. It just meant I couldn't. Life was dishing back to her in a blockbuster way what she'd dished to me.

I thought about removing the fighting spell I'd cast on her and Brent. I would have done it then and there, but I wasn't sure exactly how to reverse it. You'd think I could have made something up, but one thing magic school has taught me is that you better get your spells right or the consequences may be way worse than you'd ever foreseen. And I didn't want to cause another problem trying to erase the first one. After all, I wanted to get revenge on the little poach-crusher with a clear conscience.

That was kind of hard to plan, though, watching her cry

her eyes out on the bed where we'd talked about boys and passed countless secrets between us.

It did help when Maddie's phone rang again and she stopped crying. "Hey, Chezzie. Whassup, girl?"

Whassup, girl? Maddie *was* in bad shape to be so lame.

"Sure, come on in." Maddie sat up and wiped her eyes. "My mom's out with the boy toy. Just punch in the code and come straight up."

She hung up and ran into her bathroom. I could hear the water running, and I knew she was trying the cold-water trick to get rid of the signs of crying. When she came out of the bathroom, she looked perfect—just like the old Maddie with a mom and dad who lived together and thought she hung the moon.

Chezzie took my old place on the end of Maddie's bed and sprawled out like she'd always had that spot. Like I'd never existed. "We need to start getting ready for Nationals. Do you have any more of Pru's old routines lying around?"

"I gave you her notebook. They were all in there."

Chezzie sighed. "But what if she tries to use the new ones?"

"She won't." Maddie was sure of me. "Pru likes to stand out. To be different. She won't use any of those routines because she knows we might."

Okay, so she was right. I had always tried hard to be fresh and Prutastic—one reason I would have been the first junior head cheerleader at my old school. So Maddie still knew *me* well enough, even if I didn't recognize *her*.

To-Do started to struggle out of my back pocket. "Action step required: Study for transubstantiation test for the next two hours."

I looked at him. With a regular PDA, I could reschedule something. I'd forgotten to ask Samuel how to reschedule To-Do.

"I'm on it, To-Do." I materialized my notes, but I was paying more attention to what was going on outside the closet than on studying.

To-Do pinched my hip, unconvinced by my pretense at studying. "Action step required: Study for transubstantiation test for the next one hour and fifty-nine minutes."

"Fine!" I popped back to my room, knowing I needed a new plan. Another new plan—this one for finding time to create routines so killer, they'd get a standing O to beat all standing O's.

I was getting really good at coming up with new plans ever since we'd moved to Salem. But I was getting darned tired of it.

It was all too soon, after practicing like mortals until we were bruised and battered, that we got the chance to feel the competition magic all over again. This time, we were competing, though, not sitting in the stands. Talk about the witch-mortal divide? That's nothing compared to the spectator-performer divide. Spectators feel about one-zillionth of the adrenaline rush the performers feel. Of course, they don't—usually—end up bruised and battered, either. Thank goodness for endorphins—they keep us from feeling any pain until the day *after* the performance.

Tara clapped her hands. "Okay, Witches, I need your attention, please." After every squad on the floor knew she was head cheerleader—and only after—she turned to me and nodded. "Okay, Pru, run the girls through the drill again."

It felt great to be trusted, finally. I pulled out the book I'd done for the routine—we'd been using my drawings during practice, but they'd been bigger, glowing, and suspended against every wall in the gym so they'd be easier to read. Magic really does have its uses. But we had to use the book here in the mortal realm.

I opened the book to the first page and flipped back and forth between the first and second pages. "This is what we have planned. Everybody know what they need to do?"

It was gratifying to the max to see that everyone's eyes were on me. Tara's willingness to back the mortal practice routines had turned me from gold-plate to gold.

I'd created a few new routines for us, but there were only two that we could do reliably. Celestina still couldn't be counted on to hit her triple backflip. Which, of course, not being head cheerleader, I left to Tara. I witch-whispered to her, "You want to see how solid Celestina feels before we make the final decision on the triple-triple?"

"Hey, Celestina, how are you on the triple?" She wasn't subtle, but then again, we didn't have time for subtlety. It was competition day.

Celestina shook her head, her big brown eyes full of tears. "I don't think I can."

"Fine. You think you can hit the double-double, then that's what we'll do." Tara had decided not to risk her flubbing it. If I'd been head cheerleader, I'd have done the same. We'd like to win this, but what we really needed was the invitation to Nationals. Top five would give us that, and a triple-triple that wasn't solid could lose it for us.

"That'll make the triple-triple even more spectacular when we use it at Nationals," I said. It wouldn't be good for Celestina to feel like a loser for much longer. We had to compete with everyone on full-speed self-esteem mode.

Some of the team members might have been inclined to argue, but not here, with the crowded bleachers and the buzz of excitement that was everywhere you looked and in everything we heard.

We all felt the rush again when we got to the floor and lined up to wait for the team ahead of us to finish up. A before-competition rush is made up of five parts impatience, three parts eagerness, and two parts sheer ego. We were through the roof on the ego meter, I could see it on everyone's faces. I probably shouldn't have felt that we were golden. Whatever. I did.

"We're here again," I said, looking for even more juice. "Are we going to do it?"

Oops, I hadn't been looking at Sunita's face. She needed a boost on the ego meter, because she dared to introduce a downer vibe when it was least needed. "Maybe, if Celestina would just—"

Tara showed her head cheerleader chops with a sharp, "Hey! No negativity. Save that for Skeletor's class." Everyone laughed. Again, I felt a rush—we were in everybody mode. Which meant if I pulled my uniform skirt up and mooned the crowd, everyone on my team would laugh and think it was the kewlest move ever—until the judges tossed us out. There was nothing greater—or more dangerous—than the team phase of "everyone thinking." I was so glad we were there. I think it might have been a first for the Witches. Yay me.

Sunita said it best. "It's more exciting now that we know what to expect."

Of course, Charity, Tara's # 2 girl, was happy to chime in. "And scarier, too." This wasn't negative. When you're about to compete, the fear runs through your veins right along with everything else, fueling the perfection you're aiming for, as an individual and as a team.

Two girls responded with, "Chicken." Everyone laughed, again, which was absolutely glorious.

Charity veered into ego-ebbing territory, however, when she said, "Hey. I'm not the one who did a backflip into two people acting as bases for a flyer, now, am I?"

The guilty party—normally mild-mannered Jakeera—said, "I said sorry, and I'm the one with bigger bruises, so why are you complaining?"

I stopped all the nervous bickering with a solemn pronouncement. "We won't make any mistakes today. I can feel it in the air."

Everyone oohed. I was guru Pru today, and I liked it.

I only told the truth as I knew it, though, "Competition is going to sharpen us."

Tara said, in a rare moment of camaraderie, "I think we're pretty sharp already. When you came, it was like you stuck us into a cheer sharpener and here we are, pointy and shiny."

We all laughed, even though it wasn't exactly the best analogy ever. Like I said, that level of unity can be dangerous or powerful, depending on how it's used.

"Pru! Our cheer-whisperer." Tara held up one of my arms. "Let's do it for Pru."

Sunita asked, "Are you going to whisper to us today too?"

"Yes." Tara and I had decided we couldn't risk taking chances with everyone's confidence level.

Charity frowned. "Is that fair?"

"I think so. There's no harm in it, I'm just backing up the music cues. I can do it aloud, if you think that's more fair."

Tara shook her head. "No, aloud will sound stupid."

Charity argued with Tara, which was probably a first. I guess her ego count was going through the roof right now. "But we're doing something mortals can't do."

I pointed to the team that had just finished. "They can have headsets if they want." I shrugged. "Same thing. But maybe we should bring it to a team vote?"

Smooth Pru. I was so humble that I didn't act at all smug when the vote was unanimous: I was whispering to the team. Tara and I smiled at each other. Manage the team, safeguard the win.

Or, at least, the invitation. Our routine was solid, with some nice moments. We placed in the top five, but we hadn't quite taken the risks we needed to take first place. Or second. Or even third or fourth. I didn't like being fifth, but the team was even unhappier.

Charity complained as we waited for the other teams to clear out so we could pop home unobtrusively, "We haven't got a chance to win."

Tara fielded the complaint with a huge sigh. "We just wanted an invite to Nationals so we can compete again. We got that."

Charity huffed, "Right. We get the chance to compete— against Pru's old team, the, what, three-time champions?"

"Four," I corrected her. So she didn't like that her number-two place and her probable head cheerleadership for next year was in jeopardy. Deal with it, weeyotch.

Sunita asked, a little timidly, "Do you think we can beat your old team?"

No. But I wasn't going to say that aloud. "We can do anything if we work hard enough." Was that diplomatic enough? I hoped so. I knew the truth was deadly when we had such a short time to get up to speed before the national competition at the end of December.

Charity wasn't done being a downer, it seemed. "So can your old team, then."

"They can," I replied, since everyone already knew she was right. "And they will. Which means we need to do our best."

"I'll get that triple, Pru, I promise," Celestina said, holding up her hand to cover her heart.

"Great!" And it was, too. You had to know what you had to beat if you wanted a chance to do well in competition. Pulling off a triple-triple would give us a leg up, so to speak, on the difficulty level.

As I popped back home, to the living room where Dorklock was playing his video games, Dad was working on his next big ad campaign on the laptop, and Mom was reading, I wondered whether Chezzie and Maddie had bothered to check the results and were worried about us—or whether they thought we'd just be a good laugh.

Dad looked up from his laptop. "Hi, princess. How did the team do?"

"We were in the top five, so we got our invite to Nationals."

"Doesn't that mean you'll have to go up against your old team?"

Duh. "I guess so." No way did I want him to guess that I was eager to grind my old team's ego into the dust—especially Maddie's. Dad was a softie about a lot of things, but friendship was not one of them. You treat your family like gold and your friends like silver, and look out if you do something petty just because you had a fight.

Mom intervened before he could give me a lecture. "I'm sorry about that, Pru, but I suppose there isn't anything you can do about it. You have a new team to work with now."

Apparently, Dad saw the logic of that. Which was great— because it was his fault, and Mom's, that I'd had to switch teams in the first place.

It occurred to me that if I really wanted to know what Maddie was saying about me, I could find out. All I'd need to do was pay her a little visit every now and then before Nationals wearing my *très* chic invisibility bubble—the fashion must for any good gossip spy/witch. I'd perfected it for the test I'd had to take to get out of remedial classes. Even though I hadn't needed it for the test, I knew it would still come in handy someday.

Besides, if Dorklock could do it, I knew I had to—no way was my little brother going to run rings around me with his magic for long.

Chapter 7

Mr. Bindlebrot kept me after class. Sure, he's Orlando Bloom hot, but my former crush on him is cold, so I was not feeling the love as he stood there looking at me with disappointment.

"Pru, you missed the test on Friday while you were helping Coach Gertie with the pep rally. You need to make it up quickly if you want the grade in by the end of term."

"I will." I pulled out To-Do, hoping to score a few teacher points and lighten the disappointment in his eyes. "When can we reschedule?"

"Today. Right after school."

To-Do shook his Troll doll swath of hair. "I'm afraid that time is already scheduled. You have practice after school, a study session for transfiguration directly after practice, a tutoring session on scrying after that, and—"

Sigh. So much for points for being organized. "When *do* I have free time?"

To-Do grumped and groaned a bit as he searched his data banks. "June sixteenth is free."

Of course it was. That was the first day of summer break.

Mr. Bindlebrot frowned. "Pru, this test is very important. If you don't do well, you will fail the term."

"I know." I hadn't really known, but no way was I going to confess that to the man who held my grade in his hand. "I'm still getting used to this whole magic curriculum idea." I smiled. I so needed him on my side. "Math used to be one of my easy subjects, Mom always said." It was a little sneaky using the Mom card—she and Mr. B had been classmates way back in the Dark Ages (technically, more like the Middle Ages, but still, it was so long ago, they not only didn't have iPods, they didn't have indoor plumbing).

I stuck To-Do back in my pocket. "I'll juggle my schedule around the makeup test. Just tell me when."

"I'll give you some time to clear that busy schedule of yours. How about Monday? Directly after school."

"Great. I'll be there. And I'll ace the test." Which meant scheduling in study time as well as test time. To-Do would grumble, but he'd handle it.

Our next game after Regionals was a mortal game. We were stoked about getting an invitation to Nationals, but Tara and I were even more stoked that we were playing Angelo's school. I'd arranged with Angelo that we'd go get burgers after the game. It was a way to keep completely off the parent radar—witch and mortal. Angelo's mom would probably pitch a fit if she knew that he was seeing Tara. Tara's parents—they'd pitch a fit that might level a town if they found out their daughter was seeing a mortal boy.

First, however, we had decided that we needed to prepare killer routines for the games. There's something about practice that makes even the most wowalicious routines seem less than fab. An audience to wow? That adds sparkle to the simplest cheer, and gives our football players the spirit to crush the opposition.

Not that our team needs much spirit. The cheerleaders at Angelo's school were okay, but their football team was much worse than ours. That could have gotten messy, if Angelo cared about football. There's nothing that will ditch a romance faster than rival football rooting.

Fortunately, Angelo was so nonchalant about the game that he even hung out on our side of the field, which had its upside (eye-candy factor in the double digits) and its downside (eye-candy factor in the double digits means cheerleaders who are paying attention to the eye candy rather than the routine or the game).

As head cheerleader, Tara was a bad person to have distracted during our game. But you'd never have known she'd given the score or the play on the field a thought, the way she interrupted every move to wink at Angelo. Anyone in the stands could see that every bounce and kick and flip was aimed right at him. He, being sixteen, ate it up with a fork and two spoons.

I have to be honest: I know what Tara sees in Angelo, but I don't have a clue what Angelo sees in Tara. At first, when I got them together for some playacting at the Old Salem Village on Halloween, I didn't think he was that into her. But now I don't know. I wasn't the happiest to see them flirting. But that was nothing compared to the unhappiness of the other cheerleaders. And noncheerleaders.

"Does it ever bother you the way girls keep looking over at you?" I asked him while we were on break—a much-needed break for his side, because our football team was making short work of theirs. I didn't mention his team's poor performance to Angelo, because it was his school, but I actually wondered if this would be the first football game to last not much more than the one hour set on the clock at the start of the game. "Are you this popular at all the games?"

"No." He seemed embarrassed by the attention, but not surprised. "I'm not that into sports." He held up his hands belatedly, realizing that he was talking to cheerleaders. "No offense."

Tara laughed. Tara—the cheerleader who once released a bloodcurdling scream on the sidelines of a game because someone in the bleachers leaned down to say, "Cheerleading, the sport of pigeons!" while we were cheering on our team.

I shrugged, looking at the way that the girls—never mind girls, there were middle-aged, double-chinned women staring at him. Creepy. "Yeah, you're more into gardening and studying, right?" No wonder he liked the solitary pursuits. I thought of the times I had sat at my window and watched him rake our yard or mow our lawn. Did I look as moony as these girls? I hoped not.

"I guess you could say that. At least, until I can get out west and start making films."

He'd told me that before—that he wanted to be an actor. I hadn't been sure he'd actually get his chance, though—his mom was a bit on the bossy side, and she wanted him to go to Harvard and be a doctor. "How do you know that film-making is really what you want, anyway?"

He shrugged. "I don't. All I *am* sure of is that I want to grow up and get my mom out of my business so I can figure out what I really want." He grinned, an infectious grin that I felt in my toes. Then he looked at Tara and said, "Right, babe?" *Gah*.

One of the other team's cheerleaders wandered over to our side of the field. I didn't have to wonder what brought her past enemy lines without thought of consequence. She was staring straight at Angelo and smiling a bright smile only a truly happy cheerleader can manage. "Hey, Angelo."

"Hey, Nadia." He wasn't totally clueless. He glanced quickly at Tara and moved close enough to sling an arm around her so that anyone would know they were an item.

Anyone but this Nadia girl, I guess. "We have a bet going, and I'm supposed to find out who's the winner. Who did you ask to the winter dance?" She glanced at Tara with an expression that said, "clearly not this weeyotch."

Angelo gave an answer that made Tara smile. "I didn't ask anyone because I'm not going to be able to go. I have to work." This wasn't true. Angelo did yard work. Not much call for it after dark, and it got dark here at, like, three o'clock in the winter. But when he'd asked Tara, we'd realized there was no way to cover up enough to make sure her parents didn't find out.

Angelo had been cool about the whole freaked-out-parent thing, probably because his mother was head of the parental freak-out club. Tara and I were still trying to brainstorm a way for her to go, though. If not to the winter dance, then to the prom. She really wanted to go to a mortal prom. But it wouldn't be easy because the parents, and the school, had placed alarm charms in every mortal school way back when a few witch kids decided to expand the rather narrow dating pool into the mortal realm. The charms were not triggered by games and competitions, only by individual students being where they didn't belong. Like Tara, with Angelo, at a dance.

"Oh, too bad you can't call in sick." The Nadia girl waited a beat, to see if he'd ditch his nonexistent job and invite her. He didn't, so she shrugged. "I guess I win, then. I said you didn't ask anyone."

The most bizarre thing of all was that this girl acted like it was not at all unusual for random girls to dash their hopes up against the Angelo rock without losing hope for the next time. She turned to me and said, "That double-step double-flip thing you guys do is the bomb."

I was glad she'd taken her eyes off Angelo long enough to notice. "Thanks."

Clearly, she wasn't just being polite and standing there for a minute so her teammates wouldn't think she'd gotten the Angelo brush-off too quickly. "Do you have your own choreographer?"

I was probably a little teensy bit full of myself, since we were still on our regional invitation win high. "Just me." Then I looked over to see if Tara was going to get her hair in a ruffle over the truth. But, no. She was way too busy looking at Angelo.

"Wow." She probably would have asked more, but the buzzer sounded and she had to go back to her side of the field.

As we did our new kick-kick-backflip routine, I wondered

how long it would be before the other team would be imitating it. In cheerleading, imitation is definitely the best flattery—as long as we had moved on to the next routine before the less imaginative teams decided to steal our old routines.

When our team finally creamed their team, we leaped and cheered and roused the crowd into a roar.

Angelo was still there, on the enemy side of the field. I couldn't help teasing him. There was just something about the way he looked that made me want to see his dimple appear and a little shy flush sneak into his cheeks. I couldn't do a full-on flirt with him, like I really wanted to do, but this was second best. "How does it feel to be a traitor to your school?"

"Hey, only one more year and I'll be done. Then it won't be my school anymore." He added, "I guess I never felt like I belonged. Mom says most high school kids say that. But she did ask me if I wanted to go to your school when you guys moved in. I think she likes you." He gave me a smile, which was way too dangerous. Especially since I knew exactly what he meant about not fitting in at school.

Fortunately, before I could do something stupid, Tara walked over to us, eyeing me in a way that asked if I was chasing her guy.

I looked back, with a gaze that said, "I'm no guy poacher." At least, not if I can help it.

Angelo ignored the subtext between us. Or maybe he was

so used to it, he didn't notice. I was beginning to notice, now that it wasn't just him and me bonding over a glass of water and some leaf raking, that he was not comfortable with how strongly other females came on to him. He tended to say something to deflect the situation, like now, when he said, "Ready to get our burgers?"

"After this routine? I'm starved." Tara looked at me, and I looked at her. She so did not want me to join them.

Some of my concern about getting on her bad side had lessened once she had a personal diss-debt to settle with Chezzie. Still, why push my luck?

Then I made the mistake of looking at Angelo. Somehow, when he was smiling at me like that, I really didn't want to say no. So I didn't.

Besides, I was starving too, and a burger with Tara and Angelo was better than a snack at my house, with Mom quizzing me about how the game went and how school was going. Or worse, now that she was interim librarian, she had taken to asking me questions about random kids she'd met in the library. Like I was going to dish on another kid to my mom. As if.

In the burger joint, girls—and the waitress who had jowls on her jowls and must have been seventy—were staring at Angelo again.

"You sure are popular," I teased him. It may have been a warning to Tara not to get too comfortable thinking of

Angelo as hers, too. But not a big zappy warning. More of a tiny buzz kind of warning.

"Right." He laughed, not looking at the girls who were staring at him. "For a popular guy, I always feel different from everyone else." He didn't look at me, just concentrated on munching on fries. I don't think he talked about this much with other people. Which gave me a nice warm feeling inside that had nothing to do with my hot apple cider.

"Me too," said Tara.

I took a bite of my jalapeño burger and just nodded. Different. He had no idea what it felt like to be different in two different worlds. I mean, I was different in the mortal world because I'm a witch, and in the witch world because I lived like a mortal for sixteen years.

I don't think he could top that one, just because he had a little extra zap of Hottie Factor #9.

When I went to the ladies' room, Tara followed me. "You need to get lost, Pru."

"I know, I know. Make my excuses, okay?" I pretended I was going to pop out and then I stopped like I'd just thought of something. "Wait. That's not going to work. We were all going to go to my house after. Remember?"

"Plans can change."

Read: Plans better change if I wanted to stay on Tara's good side.

"Fine." I sighed heavily as we went back to the table, but I was ready to roll with the sideline punch. I couldn't help jabbing back at Tara, though. She had to see him on the down low from her parents. Which until tonight had meant at my house. A studying with friends kind of date, if you will.

"I have to go." I started getting my stuff together. "You guys coming to my house as usual?"

"Sure." Angelo started to get his stuff together.

"Maybe." Tara picked up a cold fry and nibbled on it daintily. "But why don't you go on ahead and we'll catch up. I'm not done with my fries yet."

"I promised your mom I'd trim the dead branch off the tree by the side of the house," Angelo said, with a cute little "forgive me" smile to Tara. Round and match to Angelo. And me.

I smiled at them and slid out of the booth. "Right, then, see you later. I've got homework to do."

I always had homework to do. Hanging with Angelo was always kewl, even if Tara was there. But I didn't have a lot of downtime to hang out with anything but the family spell book and a whole bunch of icky ingredients that combine to make potions, forecast the future, and scry the globe.

Which was something Tara counted on—me out of the room sneaking in some study time while she had Angelo to herself. So she wasn't even all that mad at me when she came in. She caught me floating in midair upside down trying to figure out exactly how an upside-down floating pyramid would work for a witch game. "No mortal alert needed," she said cheerfully. "Angelo's outside, to trim that tree for your mom." She looked at the routine I had outlined on the wall above the fireplace. "Neat. Do you think that one will take long to learn?"

"Nope. It's pretty simple, but it looks spectacular." Or at least it had the potential to—I wouldn't know until I actually saw it executed in practice.

Tara wandered over to the window to spy on Angelo. "Mortals are strangely attractive, don't you think? How did you ever manage to get any work done at school when there were so many all around you?"

"Most of them aren't like Angelo." Which was completely true. Angelo had this strange ability to make you look at him as if he glowed. Don't get me wrong—he's eye candy of the first order. But when he looks right at you, everything dials up a notch. I was kind of glad it wasn't just me, but Tara and lots of other girls who were affected as well.

Mom came in and pretended to check through the mail. Like mortal mail was that important. Dad did all the important bill stuff online and he had since before we moved here. She just wanted an excuse to listen to our conversation, but she didn't want to feel guilty for using magic to eavesdrop. Subtle, Mom. The going-back-to-work exhaustion had left her, which meant she was no longer too tired to burrow into my business—and Dorklock's, too—like she'd done before the whole work-at-Agatha's-and-ruin-my-rep thing.

I wished she didn't always listen in. To be honest, though, the couple of weeks when she hadn't had felt weird. She's always up in my business, ever since I was born. Says it's part of the job.

"Would you girls like some cider and pumpkin bread?"

"No thanks, Mom. We just ate."

"I'm stuffed. I had way too many fries." Tara hadn't quite gotten used to the way my mother hovered in a very mortal and very nonwitch mom way. "Thank you for asking, Mrs. S."

Angelo came in from trimming the tree with a pine cone for each of us, and I forgot about Mom. As long as she didn't try to give us advice about Angelo like she was a girlfriend, I could live with her hearing more than I thought she should hear about my life and my friends.

Tara went all girlie girl about the pine cone. I did too, even though I knew deep down that it was an overreaction.

The weird thing was, he brought one to Mom and she blushed.

"Are you blushing, Mom?" I witch-whispered to her in horror. "He's a kid and you're . . . old!"

She smiled as if she hadn't heard me. I doubt Tara or Angelo noticed anything when she asked, "Can I get you three some cider or some banana bread? I just made it." But I could see how she looked very hard at Angelo when he happily agreed to banana bread. And then at us, when Tara and I parroted that we'd love some too.

Chapter 8

At practice, we were short one girl. Charity. I shouldn't have been uneasy, but I was. Sure, she could be sick, or busy. But even Tara didn't look happy. We needed every girl at every practice from now until Nationals if we wanted a chance to win.

Coach Gertie blew her whistle to stop us from standing there and gossiping about it. "I'm afraid Charity may not have permission to cheer with us any longer. She and her parents are discussing the situation with Agatha right now."

"What will we do if she can't?" There was a general buzz full of this question, so Coach Gertie raised her hands to put a silencing spell on us.

"Girls, please let me speak. And then you may ask your

questions." She looked at Tara. "I know this isn't ideal, but we do have some alternates on the list. We can call them in if needed."

Then she faced us all and said very gravely, "I have a question for all of you. I'm going to ask it, and then I'm going to raise the silence spell. When I do, please answer one by one in the order in which you are standing. Understood?"

We nodded.

"Excellent." She sighed heavily and then asked, "Have any of your parents noticed your bruises and asked about how you got them? Or have you shared with them that we are practicing like mortals?"

She lifted the bubble and, shocked by the question and all of its implications, we answered her briefly, just as she asked. Most of the team hadn't mentioned a word, or been asked by their parents. Sunita's parents had asked her how she'd gotten her bruise and she'd just said practicing a great new cheering routine.

Tara witch-whispered to me, "Charity complained to her parents about the binding spell Coach Gertie casts during practice. I know she did. I was there."

Great. This was trouble. Big trouble. Not that we could do anything about it.

Coach Gertie blew her whistle. "Okay, girls. Go ahead and practice. I'll take Charity's place if you need an extra body."

We were all completely dumbstruck at that one. But what do you say to your coach?—"Gee thanks, Coach, but have you done a backflip in the last century?"

Fortunately, our silence made Coach laugh. "Don't worry girls, I'll be using magic. I'm just a stand-in."

I was nervous, but there was no reason. With our powers bound, but Coach Gertie using her magic, the routine went even more smoothly than it had with Charity. We nailed the whole routine. A first for us, for practice. Usually you don't hit perfect until you're on the field, or the competition floor. Something about having an audience, I guess.

One of the lessons I've had to learn over and over again: Just when you think you'll never get it, you do. You'd think, "I have that down," but you never do until the moment you know you've got it. And then, for about thirty seconds, you do.

Like when our practice turned into perfection. Okay, Sunita almost fell once, but perfect is a relative term when it comes to the Salem Witches.

And perfection is when we all end a routine with a moment of stunned silence, and then leap around and scream, "We did it."

Synchronicity. No doubt about it.

"Excellent practice, girls." Coach Gertie even replayed it for us in slow motion, although she blurred her own form out, saying, "Don't need to see that, now, do we?"

We had a brilliant routine, a few bruises, and mucho excitement.

"Now," I said, and stepped up to the next part of my plan. "We do this as witches."

This was not news to Tara, but I still caught her by surprise. "What do you mean?"

I probably should have warned her, but the whole Charity thing had really rocked me. "I've written up some great routines for Saturday's magic game."

"Saturday?" Tara didn't like my taking the polish off her happy crown. "We don't have time to add new routines."

"They're simple—they just need us to show this same kind of timing. They'll be great."

"I don't know."

"Well, we can try them, can't we?" Sunita whispered her question, but we all stared at her, amazed she had volunteered any opinion at all.

Coach Gertie smiled. "That's the attitude I'm looking for in my champions."

We started getting the buzz back. Champions. After nailing the practice with three new routines, we were ready and almost willing to believe.

Celestina looked at me, and then, quickly realizing her mistake, turned to Tara. "Do you really think we can win?"

Tara looked at me, her eyes narrowed, and I knew she was going to hold a grudge against me for a little while. "Maybe."

Oh well, Tara could hold a grudge, but I wasn't about to let it bring me down. "Hey, no maybes allowed until after the competition!"

Tara wasn't happy with me setting any rules or pronouncements. "What do you mean? Maybe is maybe."

"From now until after competition, maybe is for losers, like Chezzie's going to be." I wasn't a complete fool; I reminded her what the stakes were. "Winners know they're going to win. They don't say maybe."

Celestina, rather unhelpfully, asked, "What do winners do when they lose?"

I looked at her an extra-long second before answering, hoping to discourage any other loser-type questions. "Figure out why and make sure it doesn't happen again, of course."

She smiled a little shakily. "Of course."

I didn't like the lack of enthusiasm. "Let's try that again. Are there any maybes left after that practice?"

"No."

"Are we going to win?"

"Yes!" All of us, at the same time, set off streamers, confetti, a few fireworks, and glimmering lights. Synchronicity. What a beautiful thing.

The practice had gone pretty well. There had been just one teensy glitch: I'd missed my makeup exam with Mr. Bindlebrot. And he wasn't happy about it.

"I'm sorry, Pru. The term is over. I have to have grades in today, and any corrections or updates in a week. There's nothing I can do."

"Extra credit?" I begged. I pleaded.

He relented. "You could create an exhibit to explain sine/cosine to future classes."

Sure. I had lots of time to do an exhibit. "By Friday?"

He rubbed his eyes as if he were tired, despite the fact that it was only nine in the morning. "By Friday."

"Great!"

"Pru." He looked at me seriously, like he was going to drop a bombshell. "If the exhibit is good, you'll pass. But until then, you have a failing grade for the term."

Kaboom.

"I understand." Sure, I did. I'd have plenty of time to make an A+++ exhibit. I was suspended from the cheerleading team until I'd cleared the F from my permanent record.

I put the whole suspension thing out of my mind as soon as I put the extra-credit project in To-Do. Tara hadn't been too happy when I'd broken the news to her—until I pointed out that I could still write routines for the team, I just couldn't go to practice until Mr. Bindlebrot approved the extra credit project.

"Just hurry up," she warned. "We need the whole team in form. Especially you."

It was nice to hear that, but this me versus me battle of the cheering giants was getting on my nerves. I had created a few new routines, but would they be good enough? I hadn't had a chance to pop in and spy on Maddie and Chezzie again. To-Do was a bully when it came to action steps being performed on time.

It was critical that I know what Maddie and Chezzie were planning. But I also needed to study, practice, and come up with some killer competition routines for the squad. I knew what I needed. I just didn't have a second to spare in my already full schedule. I wished, not for the first time, that turn-back-time spells were not prohibited for use by minors without adult supervision. Still, there must be some magic, somewhere, that could help me. That's where Samuel came in.

When Samuel arrived to tutor me, I had the family spell book in front of me. I had discovered that when I did that, he would always say . . .

"Hi. What do you need in there?"

Like clockwork. Beats searching through a dusty spell book, which I've found is kind of like looking for a typo in a dictionary.

I tried to look as innocent as possible without looking so innocent, I morphed into guilty-by-reason-of-innocence. "I need a tracking spell." I held my breath, hoping he wouldn't say they, too, were out-of-bounds for minors.

Happily, he said, "Piece of cake." He stopped for a second, looking puzzled. "For what class?"

"An extra-credit project." I'd made the excuse up in advance. I did have extra-credit projects, but not this one.

The wrinkles in his forehead went away, and he moved on to yet another question I wished I didn't have to answer. "What do you need to track?"

Oooh. Trickier question. No way was I going to tell him I wanted to track mortals. Who would he be less likely to do a red alert on? Aha! "Dorklock."

"Why would a teacher want you to—"

"I'm just supposed to track his movements for twenty-four hours straight. You know, video games, dinner, school—that stuff. A kid is safer to track than an adult."

"Either's a piece of cake."

"For you, maybe." I frowned at him. Sometimes I hated that he always knew so much more than I did and never even tried to hide it from me. Geek. "Besides, you need a new saying. That one was old before our mothers were born."

He winced a little, reminding me that his mother was dead. Oops. I tried to pry my foot out from between my teeth. "How about 'piece of tritium'?"

His eyes lit up at my use of a scientific word. I hoped he didn't think that was going to become a habit. "That could work. But really, you'd need—"

Oh, no. If I didn't stop him, we'd be talking science for a year. I grabbed To-Do out of my back pocket and held him up. "Stop!"

To-Do blinked and said, "Action step: Tutoring session with Samuel; remaining time fifty-six minutes."

I stuffed To-Do back into my pocket. "Let's keep focused here, okay? I need a tracking spell for Dorklock."

It was, like Samuel had said, a piece of cake. Or tritium, maybe. We created a charm with one of Dorklock's dirty socks. I figured I could copy the charm with an old lip gloss of Maddie's I had stuck in a purse and had never thrown out. That way, he'd never be the wiser that it was Maddie I *really* intended to track. I didn't fall off the pyramid yesterday, by any means.

The spell we attached to the charm was pretty simple:

"Thread to me
Spatial energy
When tap I
A tap of three."

After the spell was bound to the charm, I could tap the sock and it would instantly show me wherever Dorklock was. It would even buzz helpfully if he was close by. "You were right. This wasn't hard at all." Although, next time, I'd have to consider my charm source more carefully.

Dorklock's sock really reeked and was no doubt toxic to the touch. Good thing I didn't really want to track him.

"It's harder with people you don't know," he said, flipping his glasses at me, which meant he was nervous. "I thought you might have meant to track Daniel."

"I don't have anything of his," I said quickly, to shut down that whole jealous thing Samuel has going about Daniel. But then I remembered the card Daniel popped into my room on Thanksgiving. No way did I want to get into how intriguing I found it to think I might actually be able to track Daniel down somewhere. Not that I needed any more action items on my to-do list right now.

"Right." He looked relieved. "Good. Because he's nothing but trouble."

I frowned back, annoyed. Why did boys have to be so possessive, even when they were just best friends? "Thanks, like I couldn't guess that since he nearly got me expelled from school. I'm interested in honing my own skills, not finding some Prince Witchling to save the day for me. I *would* like to be able to figure out this stuff on my own, one day, you know. Unless you plan to keep tutoring me until I'm, like, five hundred and sixty."

He flipped his glasses at me, speechless.

Oops, I'd been joking and accidentally got myself into dangerous territory. I quickly added, before he could weigh in on whether or not he'd like to be tutoring me for half a millennium, "I hoped part of the reason why I got it so quickly was because I was getting better at this whole magic thing." I kept going, waiting for the red flush to leave his cheeks. Neither one of us really wanted him to say something embarrassing. "It's bad enough that I have to scramble and rely on a Troll doll to keep up right now. But to spend my whole senior year studying and worrying about grades? What a waste of the last year of high school."

He relaxed a bit, and grinned. "The way you're going, you'll be the one tutoring me next year."

I laughed. It was funny, and exactly the sweetly absurd thing Samuel would say. The only thing I could tutor him on was dressing well and having just a little bit more social polish. We both knew that—and we both knew he wasn't interested in that kind of tutoring.

Besides, I didn't want him to know I hoped he was right, that I wouldn't need him as a tutor next year. Boys were a confusing issue right now. There was Daniel, Agatha's great-to-the-nth grandson, who had run away but still occasionally sent me anonymous notes that weren't anonymous to me. There was Angelo: mortal, off-limits, and totally scrumptious. And Samuel: geek extraordinaire and all-around nice guy. Sure, there was some mystery there, about how his mom died and why he lived with his dad, but he was just my best friend. Nothing more, even if he did kind of get under my skin with those puppy dog eyes of his.

I couldn't afford to explore any of those possibilities, though. Not if I wanted to pass all my classes and make sure the Witches crushed my old team at the national competition. Better just to smile and avoid all the boy-girl traps that are set everywhere—school, home, and in the daily conversations of my team members.

Okay, truthfully, it wasn't better. Better would be to run away from school and spend all my free time learning everything I could about boy-girl dynamics. The only downside to that would be that I wouldn't get to see the Witches beat my old team.

So maybe I could wait to run away until after Nationals.

But first—I waved my hand and made the beginning of my extra-credit math project appear in the air. A sine symbol. "I forgot to tell you. I need to get this extra credit done for Mr. Bindlebrot ASAP. Can you help?"

Chapter 9

Mr. Bindlebrot stared at my extra-credit project. "Very impressive, Pru."

"So? Do I pass?"

He smiled and rubbed the bridge of his nose, like I do when I have a headache. "Let me take a look and see. I'll let you know."

"But—"

He sighed. "Pru. Give me a week. Your extra credit wasn't in my schedule any more than it was in yours. Okay?"

"Okay." *Not.* But he was the teacher. And I needed that grade.

I showed up at practice a few minutes late. Not that it mattered. Tara spotted me right away and flew over with a smile. "Bindlebrot pass your extra credit?"

"He wants a week."

"A week!" She settled to the floor next to me. "What are you doing here, then? You can't come to practice if—"

"I know." I handed her a stack of routines I'd sketched out. "I just wanted to give you the 411 and these new routines."

I looked at the girls practicing. "And don't worry. If I can't practice with the team, I can spy for you." I told her about my tracking spell for Maddie and Chezzie.

"What have you found out?"

"Nothing yet. I've been too busy doing the extra-credit project."

Like a good HC, she nodded and flicked her hand at me. "Well, get to it, then."

Unfortunately, the tracking spell was a dud. When I touched the charmed lip gloss, I got . . . a thin film of purse lint on my fingertip. Samuel wasn't one to do poor magic, though, so I figured I was doing something wrong.

I would have tried to figure it out, but To-Do whistled, to remind me that it was time for my scrying homework. I was tempted to see if I could spy into the future and see if Mr. B was going to give me a passing grade, but I only had enough time to do the assigned homework: gaze deeply into the crystal and find out whether it would snow in Tahoe at 10:43 p.m. tonight. Sigh.

On Saturday morning, since I couldn't cheer and was forbidden even to attend the game as a spectator, I decided to skip the pedicure appointment I badly needed and figure out what was wrong with the Maddie-tracking charm. Dorklock's sock had gone toxic, so I grabbed the first thing that came to hand—Samuel's lucky rock that he'd left to help me get an A on my extra credit.

I really wasn't trying to spy on him. I just meant to see if I could get the spell to work. But after I touched the lucky rock and saw—I had to go and check it out.

I arrived at the mortal grocery store discreetly, just in time to see him carrying a bag of groceries to the car for the frail-looking mortal woman beside him.

I walked up to him and said, "Hi, Samuel." This was, as I well knew, a proven technique to find out if someone is doing something they're not supposed to be doing. Most of my classmates' mothers—and a few fathers—used it routinely to make sure the secretary/pool boy/maid/plumber was not going above and beyond the call of duty, if you get my drift.

Samuel's reaction was pretty much into the red zone of the guilt-meter. He looked at me as if I were an alien bug with waving tentacles and a hungry dripping maw, like in the *Alien* movies. I assumed it was the fact I was a witch, and so shouldn't be fraternizing with mortals. Not that the old lady would know if we didn't tell her. Besides, Samuel was here. So, really, what's the big deal? I might have witch-whispered the question, but I didn't have time.

"Is this the young lady who has been cutting into our

time, Sammy?" the old lady teased, her eyes twinkling as she assessed me.

Oh. So that was the big deal. *Sammy* was consorting with mortals for some reason. And this particular mortal knew him well enough to ask embarrassing questions.

"We're just friends," I said as quickly as possible without being impolite.

She smiled and looked at Samuel. "Don't lose hope. The good ones are always hard to catch."

Oh, great. Samuel had hooked up with a mortal who not only called him Sammy, but who was a matchmaker wannabe, too.

"I just wanted to ask a quick question about some homework," I said.

"Well, Sammy was going to come in for cookies and tea, so I can thank him for weeding my flower beds this morning."

Weeding flower beds? In the winter? Did this lady have Alzheimer's?

"I'll catch up with you later, Pru." Samuel wanted me gone, which raised my radar big-time.

I would have walked away, though, if the old lady hadn't said, "I'm Nina Sutton-Pierce, young lady, and you are certainly welcome to join us."

I stuck out my hand. "Prudence Stewart. I'd be delighted." I didn't add that my delight grew more when I saw Samuel was glaring at me. Or that my curiosity included a bit of worry that my best friend was doing something that was going to get him in trouble if anyone ever found out.

"I'm sure Pru has better things to do. She's a busy girl."

"Nonsense. I insist. You're wonderful company, dear boy, but I am in the mood for a nice girl-to-girl chat. We girls just know how to talk, don't we?"

I nodded. Samuel rolled his eyes at me, careful not to let Ms. Sutton-Pierce notice.

She lived in a little one-bedroom house on a neat square patch of well-kept lawn. Each window held a flower box full of colorful flowers I couldn't even begin to name. It was winter, and I wondered how they were blooming until I realized they were fake.

She saw me notice and smiled. "I like a year-round garden, but living in Massachusetts, I must resort to artifice some months. Sammy weeds the real garden in the spring and summer. For these, he pulls out the dead leaves and the street trash that sometimes blows into my window boxes in the fall and winter. And washes off the dust, to keep them looking fresh."

That was a lot of work for some fake flowers, but I didn't think either of them would appreciate my saying so. "They're beautiful."

"Thanks to this fine young man." She smiled at Samuel. "It's not every one his age who'll come by to check on an old woman every week."

Samuel seemed to be worried that I was going to freak at that news. Didn't he know I already knew he was a mortal groupie? Better he help out lonely old ladies than hit on girls who might be susceptible to a not-very-chivalrous seduction charm. Not that I could imagine Samuel and seduction in the same paragraph, never mind the same sentence.

We had tea, we had a nice chat. We even got in some girls-only time while Samuel fixed her toaster because it had been burning her morning toast. If she'd been a few decades younger, I'd have sworn he had a major crush. But I could understand why he liked her. She was funny, and sweet, and there was a kind of light around her when she told me how much she appreciated the way I paid attention to an old lady as if I were interested—and when she laughed and told me she appreciated my sweetness when I assured her that I was not pretending. Even though it was the truth.

It wasn't until we said good-bye and left—through the front door, walking down the street like mortals while she waved to us from her window—that Samuel really let me know how mad he was. Anyone who didn't know him probably wouldn't have guessed that the way he didn't talk to me, or didn't look at me when he started walking away, was not just a geeky lack of manners.

"Why so mad?" I said to his stiff-shouldered back. "She's a kewl old lady. I'm not going to rat you out to Agatha. How you get your mortal groupie fix is no one else's business."

He stopped walking. His shoulders were so tense, I could see that he wasn't sure whether he should turn around or not, but he did. "You liked her?"

Duh. What wasn't to like? "Of course I did."

"I do too." He flipped the tri-lenses of his glasses until I wanted to rip the glasses off his nose and toss them into the street. Finally, he whispered, "And I don't want her to get hurt."

Whoa. He wasn't kidding. He was really afraid. Samuel wasn't a rule-breaker for the most part—unless the rule didn't make sense or follow a clear and logical path. Which meant I whispered back when I asked, "Would the witches' council do something to her just because you're her knight-in-shining-toolbelt every week?"

He shook his head. "No, they wouldn't hurt her. She's no harm to them."

"Then what's the big deal? When I was in Beverly Hills we used to go visit an old-folks home every Christmas. It's called volunteering in your community. It's a good thing."

"Sure it is." For some reason, he was still upset. "But the witches' council might tell my dad to make me stop seeing her. She doesn't have anyone else. She'd miss me."

Wow. He was very attached to his community project. I held up my hands to indicate surrender. "I get it. I'm not planning to say anything."

"Good." I guess he'd decided to trust that I wasn't trying

to get him—or the old lady—in trouble. Or at least forgive me, because he smiled and turned back into the Samuel I was more familiar with. "So, why did you want to find me in the first place?"

There was still a shadow of a secret in the way he looked around nervously as he talked to me. I decided to let it go. I could worm it out of him later, when he wasn't so worried that I would spill his stupid secret. So he was the witch version of a Boy Scout, helping out an old lady. So what? I didn't have time for his boy drama. I had girl drama to take care of. "This tracking spell isn't working for me."

He crossed his arms and looked at me. "Could have fooled me."

Okay, so that had sounded stupid. "I tracked you, but I can't track . . . Dorklock." He looked even more skeptical. Sometimes I wish I didn't have such smart friends. I couldn't get away with anything that would have flown like a kite in Beverly Hills. I sighed. "Anyway, can you help me figure out what I'm doing wrong?"

"Okay." He stared at me for a second, though, as if he was thinking how to say, "First, promise me you'll never tell anyone about this."

"Are you kidding me?" What was the big deal? I had a feeling it was something juicy, but that seemed odd. Samuel wasn't the kind of guy to have juicy secrets, he had geeky ones. I knew I was going to make him mad, but I had to know. "Why would anyone else care? You're acting like you're James Bond and I'm about to blow your cover with Dr. No."

"Pru, haven't you learned anything?" I'm not sure I'd ever seen Samuel so scared. "We don't fraternize with mortals without risk."

"You'll have to forgive me if I don't see the big deal. Mom and Dorklock and I have done it for, like, my whole life."

He pounced on that. "Isn't that the whole reason you came to Agatha's? To keep your brother from doing some unintentional damage to mortals?"

"That? That was kid stuff." I don't think the council would worry that Samuel was going to puff up some old lady's skirts. Besides, she wore slacks.

"You know it isn't kid stuff." He looked at me with his puppy dog eyes again, begging me to understand. "After what happened to my mom . . ." He trailed off.

I'm not sure why I was resisting. It wasn't that big a thing to promise I wouldn't tell. Who would even care? Agatha? —umm, not my first thought for a confidante. "Fine. It's a big deal. Are you going to help me or not?"

He crossed his arms and scowled impatiently. "Are you going to promise me?"

I sighed. "Promise." I crossed my heart and said, "I hope to sprout zits if I lie."

He still didn't look happy. "I wish I could believe you,

but the more you get into the cheering stuff and the regular classes, the less I think I know you."

All I could think of was that he needed to lighten up. So I said the most absurd thing I could think of. "If you keep this up, I'm going to start to believe she's your mom and you have her hidden in the Witches' Protection Program, for goodness sake. . . ." It was my turn to trail off.

He'd turned pale. His mouth had opened and closed like a fish out of water.

My joke was maybe not so funny. Maybe it was real. Was that even possible? I squeaked out, "She *is* your mom. But, how?"

He stopped even trying to pretend. "You can't tell anyone."

I crossed my heart, totally serious this time. I didn't need to have manifested a Talent to know this was not something to take lightly. "I promise never to tell, or I'll never cheer again. But you have to tell me what happened."

Finally, he realized I wasn't fooling around. I wasn't going to tell anyone. He took a shaky breath and smiled at me a little. "She was banished. Her powers were stripped." He looked miserable. But then he shook his head, as if he was used to clearing out these kind of thoughts. He smiled again, almost back to normal. "But she's happy. So I'm happy for her. You know?"

Nope, I didn't know how he could be happy to see his mother like that. But all of a sudden it made sense. Terrible sense. If the council had banished his mom, they'd be more than a little unhappy that he'd found her and was mowing her lawn. "Does your dad even know?"

"No. He knew what her sentence meant. And he promised her he'd take care of me and not look for her." He flipped his lenses nervously. "But I didn't promise not to look for her."

"Wow. That's real Lifetime movie material." Or maybe soap opera stuff. *As the Witch Turns* or *The Bold and the Mortal.*

He winced. Sometimes I'm stupid. "Why did you go looking for her in the first place?" I asked.

"I didn't want her to be alone."

I thought about the Saturdays we'd burned up tutoring when I was trying to get out of remedial classes. "How many times did you have to cancel your 'date' with her because of me?"

"None."

"Really?" I remembered how she'd teased that her Sammy was seeing someone on the side.

"No. I always go every Saturday. I just don't stay as long."

"I'm sorry. If I'd known—"

"She would have wanted it that way. She was always on me to spend more time with friends." He shrugged. "Even if she doesn't remember, she still treats me like a mom would. Like she did when she knew she was my mom."

"Maybe you should tell your dad—" I couldn't help think how sad his dad had looked at Thanksgiving dinner.

"No way. And you can't either." He must have seen the doubt in my eyes, because he insisted. "Promise. You will not tell my dad."

"I promise. I will not tell your dad, even though I think he should know so you don't have to go through this all by yourself." I could see it wasn't easy for him, and I'd never had a clue. Impressive. Who would have thought Samuel would have a secret like this? It's a juicy one, if you like heartbreaking secrets that make you mad at powerful people. And if you're not best friends with someone who has to live with the fallout.

I didn't want to add to his pain, so I took his hand. He jumped, surprised, but I held on. "And just so you won't have any doubts, let's trade secrets, then: My silence for yours."

"What secret do you have? Everyone knows you still slip up and think like a mortal. It's part of your charm." He didn't look convinced.

I had no intention of telling him any of my super-hideous secrets, like that Daniel sent me anonymous notes. But there was one I needed to tell him, anyway, if I wanted his help. "The tracking spell I asked you to teach me? It's for tracking Maddie and Chezzie."

He shook his head. "Mortals? The girls from your old team?"

I nodded.

He whistled. "Isn't it also cheating?"

"No." I smiled. "It's just gossips gone witch."

He sighed. "Girl drama. I think I believe you. Too bad you didn't trust me in the first place. A tracking spell for mortals is just a little different from one for witches."

Maybe he was right. Maybe I should have trusted him when I asked him to teach me the tracking spell. But then I wouldn't know his secret. Now I did, which meant I could have his back. If he hadn't told his dad, he needed someone to look out for him, whether he knew it or not.

I finally heard from Mr. Bindlebrot. He'd made me sweat it for two days, but then he'd told me my extra credit had been more than enough to give me a passing grade in math. I showed up at practice ready to rumble. Tara had already told me the Witches were improving (literally) by leaps and bounds. She thought we actually had a chance to win. I wasn't sure I believed her about being ready to win Nationals—she was still a novice when it came to competition. But I did believe she could see the improvement in the team performance.

I showed up at practice happy, but my good mood didn't last long. Why is it that silver clouds have black linings? The Witches had finally managed to get ourselves to the point where we had a chance to win—and now we were forbidden.

Coach Gertie didn't look any happier than we were when she passed on the news that Agatha had forbidden her to bind our magic and banned us from mortal cheering at all. But she wasn't going to argue with Agatha.

Apparently, more than just Charity's parents had complained about the danger of our technique. "Your parents have spoken, girls. I'm sorry. You can still compete in magic games, but you are not allowed to practice or compete with mortals. Your parents feel it is too dangerous, and the headmistress has concurred."

Charity was back and looking smug. "It was stupid to try to do those lame and dangerous mortal moves. They didn't get us anything but bruised." She was truly clueless about the attitude against her in the room. "Now we can go back to the old ways."

"What are we going to do?" Tara witch-whispered to me.

I gave her a look that said "watch me" and then laughed out loud. "The old ways? I don't think so."

"You're not head cheerleader. You don't have any say." Charity frowned at me, and all the other girls looked like they hoped I'd save us all from the stupidity of clueless people like Charity.

If there weren't a charm against it on school grounds, I think Tara might have cast ice darts from her eyes straight to Charity's heart. "Pru's my second-in-command, Charity. She has a lot of say."

Charity was so shocked that she actually lost her automatic smile. "*I'm* your second-in-command."

"Don't be silly," Tara answered, with an eyebrow lift of surprise. "Why would you be my second-in-command when the winning attitude Pru has in her little toenail you don't have in your entire body, including the energy field around it?"

Charity did the gasping fish-mouth thing. Very unattractive, but particularly satisfying when we all really wanted to fillet her for messing up our plans. She looked around for a moment, as if she thought she had a friend left. Right. She gave up on that hope pretty quick and just stood there miserably, but with a mean girl challenge in her eyes while she stared at me. "What are we going to do? We can't do mortal routines. We're forbidden." She looked at Coach Gertie, who nodded unhappily.

I smiled, like I didn't want to fillet her as badly as the other girls did. It was important that I get everyone behind me. Maybe even more important than it would be on national competition day. And that was saying something. "We're going to turn our talents to a new audience."

Coach Gertie smiled at me all of a sudden. A real smile that said she suddenly thought I might be capable of getting us out of this mess. "What audience is that?" she asked.

I smiled, drawing out the suspense until I was sure all the girls were watching me. "Our parents."

There was a definite drop in the level of hope in the room. A chorus of complaints came from every direction. I singled out one I heard from at least five people: "They're never together."

"It isn't usual to find them together," I agreed. Witch parents tended to do their own thing. Kids lived with their moms and knew their dads, of course, but most witch parents protected their children by setting a lot of charms and spells over them. They were more about quality time sightseeing the globe than hands-on raising their kids. "And it won't happen naturally. But we can get them together. Remember, we can do anything, right?"

"I don't know. . . ." Even Tara wasn't quite sure.

I thought they might be more positive if I told them my idea. But I also thought it was important for them to start being positive even when things looked bleak. That's the way to get through the hard parts of competition—and life, too, I guess. So I gave them a challenge. "Maybe we should take a vote. Are we the Witches?" I held my breath, but smiled like I was sure they were all going to eagerly say yes.

"Yes." There was a surprising amount of force behind the answer, which cheered me up immensely.

"Do our parents like to see our school teams win?"

"Yes!" Great. It was unanimous. Even Charity had said yes—probably because Tara was staring her down, daring her not to. "Are we the bomb at making the impossible possible?"

"Yes!" It was practically a roar this time.

"Then let's convince our parents that we are the greatest and we deserve to cheer at Nationals!"

"Yes!" Everyone shot streamers into the air.

It turned out that getting that "Yes" was the last positive forward movement we took for a few hours. We just couldn't agree on how to get our parents' wandering attention.

I'd suggested just showing them our stuff at the next magic game. But, as was pointed out, we couldn't count on everyone to show for that. Half was probably the best we could come up with.

One group was convinced we should kidnap ourselves and plant clues so that when they came to find us, we could spring our surprise while they were still too upset to say no. Coach Gertie vetoed that one pretty quickly, to my relief. Too much *CSI* for Elektra and Sunita, I think.

Finally, I had a brainstorm that combined my idea for the next magic game with a hook that would bring out more parents. "Don't they come to awards ceremonies?" All parents come to awards ceremonies when they're told their child is going to receive an award. "Then let's pretend there's an award for best cheerleader."

At last, that idea got our positive energy flowing again. "We could send them some kewl invitations like you made for your sweet sixteen party." Elektra had really liked that party. I think she'd probably already decided to throw herself a sweet seventeen for her next birthday.

"Great." Tara was getting into it too. "And then we can beg them to come—each of us working on our own parents, of course."

Charity crossed her arms over her chest. "Mine aren't ever going to come."

Tara looked at her. "Not a problem. We'll just drop you from the team and pick an alternate."

Charity turned green, obviously shocked by the idea of being off the team.

"We don't need to be so drastic," I said to Tara, playing good cop to her excellent rendition of bad cop. "Okay, how many feel their parents are hardcore refuseniks?" Only one other girl besides Charity raised her hand.

"So let's decide what it will take to get them there, and make sure the invitation sounds like a can't-miss function." I didn't lift the threat of dropping the girls from the team who couldn't get their parents to the magic game. It was a good idea for everyone to have incentive, especially Charity.

"Girls, I think you've forgotten one thing," Coach Gertie's voice came from above our heads. We all looked up to see her floating there in her "thinking position," as she called it.

"What's that?" Tara asked.

"Your parents will not be in a cooperative mood if they arrive at the game/awards ceremony and find that there are no awards to be presented."

Okay, it was a teensy flaw in an otherwise brilliant plan. So sue me.

Coach Gertie made a goddess of herself in my eyes right then when she said, "I think we can remedy that. We'll just need to make it a true awards ceremony."

Tara was as impressed as I was. "You can do that?" And then she said, "I wish we'd thought of this sooner. No one ever appreciates what we do."

"Of course I can." Coach Gertie floated to the floor. "It's high time you girls were recognized as the serious athletes you are. So, ceremony at our next game. I'll get the word to Agatha and the other coaches. You girls make the invitations."

"Who is going to decide who gets what award?" Tara looked at me. I looked at Tara. Then we both looked at the coach.

Coach Gertie smiled mysteriously. "You girls leave that up to me. I'm the coach, after all."

Chapter 10

There's a downside to trying to keep everybody happy and all the balls in the air. For example, Tara and Angelo and I were supposed to hang out. But I needed to study for the big potions test the next day. I couldn't say anything to Angelo, of course, but alarm bells should have gone off when I saw the glint in Tara's eyes.

"It'll be okay. You can just go in and out and say you're making something in the kitchen that needs a lot of attention." She was practically drooling at the thought. "I could use some time to relax with a cute boy after all this stress about the parents going nuclear on our competition plans."

Yeah. Me too. Unfortunately, To-Do was in my back

pocket, ready to pinch me if I didn't keep to my action steps. "What do you think I could make that would need me in the kitchen constantly?"

"I have no idea. You're the one with the mother who actually cooked." She looked away from the window, where she was on Angelo-watch. "Is your mom going to come to the game?"

"Of course." Not that I was sure I wanted her there. When I'd explained everything that was going on, she hadn't been as enthusiastic as I'd expected her to be. She'd actually said, "Maybe it's for the best that you don't compete in the mortal realm for a while, honey." As if.

"Both of my parents are coming, although my dad made it sound like he was really put out, since the game isn't on one of his scheduled visiting days. But Mom says that's a put-on. He loves Dragon Ball. He used to play when he went to Agatha's." She went on red alert. "Angelo's coming. Make yourself scarce."

Sigh. "Fine. If he asks, tell him I'm making Christmas cookies. That would require me to fill pans and switch them in and out of the oven, so it shouldn't arouse his curiosity too much."

"Christmas cookies. Perfect. Don't forget to put some in the oven to bake. The house should smell like cookies. And gingerbread." Tara has a secret sweet tooth. "And Angelo and I can test them for you."

I knew I shouldn't tease her, but I couldn't help myself. "What if he wants to help make the cookies?"

She looked at me blankly, as if I'd asked if she thought Angelo might want to fly to the moon on a broomstick. "Why would he do that?"

"Because he's a nice guy, if you haven't noticed."

She grinned, a wicked grin that didn't bode well for Angelo's virtue if I left them alone too long. "It's not the 'nice' that I notice about that mortal."

No duh. "He may offer to help. If he does, I'll—"

In her best head cheerleader instruction tone, she said, "You'll say you don't need any help."

Right. "I'll say I have a system going and I promised my mom not to share our family recipes. He'll get that, since his mother is big into secrets." Secrets. That reminded me of Samuel, and his big secret. I hadn't had much time to talk to him since then. But I had sent him an invitation to the magic game. I didn't know whether to hope he came or not.

Tara shuddered. "Whatever. You understand these mortals better than I do. Not that I want to understand that woman any better."

"Yeah, well, they're a package deal. If you want Angelo, you have to tolerate his mother."

"Don't be silly." Tara smiled. "That's what I have you for: You run the best interference I've ever seen. I mean that on or off the floor."

"Gee, thanks so much." I sounded sarcastic, but I was actually a little flattered.

"Hey, we both know why I'm here. And it's not to hang out with a study-freak like you, now, is it?"

"No, it's to hide the fact you're hot for a mortal from your parents."

"Like you totally wouldn't if you weren't so busy trying to keep up in magic class."

Low blow, even if it was true. Which, I suppose, was why I didn't go back to join them as often as I should. And which was why it was my mom who noticed they were locking lips when she casually walked in to offer them something to drink.

I didn't hear any commotion. I just walked into the living room with a plate of fresh hot gingerbread to find Mom standing there, her "I'm not going to panic yet" look on her face and Tara and Angelo standing about three feet apart. They looked like they'd been pushed apart by a big wind that had also messed up their hair. Angelo's hottie factor was actually upped as he stood there with his hair standing on end, even if he also looked a little dazed and quite a bit afraid of my mom.

Tara, not knowing my mom well, tried the lying-your-way-out option. "Angelo was just trying to help me get this barrette out of my hair." She held up an ugly barrette that she'd materialized out of thin air. Even Samuel would have known that she wouldn't wear anything that hideous.

Mom didn't call her on it, though, which meant things were really bad. She just said, "I understand, Tara. But I think it's time for you to go home now."

"Sure." Tara knew when to cut her losses.

From the look in her eye as she left—through the front door, for appearances' sake—I wasn't sure if Tara was going to speak to me ever again. My mom had caught her making out with Angelo. My mom had sent her home.

Of course, after Angelo left, stumbling and red-faced, things got much worse.

It would have been awful to be punished because I was studying while they were making out—all the trouble and none of the fun. But no, my mom didn't say a word about that. Instead, she asked me three questions in that no-nonsense way of hers. And I answered them, no matter that I'd rather have waxed all the hair off my head instead.

The first question didn't seem that awful. "Do you think Tara really likes Angelo?"

"Yes." That one was easy. She was always trying to talk me into getting her more Angelo-time, so I knew she *really* liked Angelo.

"Do you really like Angelo?" That was a trickier question. But she looked me straight in the eye while she asked, and I couldn't look away.

"Yes." Admitting it aloud was a little weird. I was glad Tara wasn't there to overhear—never mind Angelo.

Mom's next question was completely out there, though. She cocked her head like she was just engaging in girl talk. "Is there a girl you know who *doesn't* like Angelo?"

"Of course—" I stopped, remembering that even Denise had kept her eye on him at my party. Denise, who always crushed on guys with tattoos or piercings, or both. "No."

She sighed, as if my answers were very bad news. "Okay. I'll be back in a minute."

"Why? What are you going to do? This isn't Angelo's fault." I had a bad feeling in the pit of my stomach.

Nothing, however, prepared me for what my mother said right before she popped out of the room, "Of course it is, honey. But I don't think he can help it. Maybe it's not too late. If Agatha will take him into the school."

Yep. My mom went nuts just because Tara and Angelo made out in the living room. So nuts, she was going to try to convince Agatha to take Angelo into the school. A mortal. Being interviewed by the mortal-disdaining headmistress of a school for witches. I remembered my interview with Agatha. I wouldn't wish that on my worst enemy, never mind Angelo.

There was sooo much wrong with this that I couldn't even begin to deal with it. To-Do pinched my hip. "Study for scrying midterm to begin now." I summoned the scrying crystal and buried myself in my homework, glad to have something to distract me from the disaster that had just occurred. Until I smelled cookies burning.

I was headed back to the kitchen to rescue the Christmas cookies that Angelo was never going to eat when someone called my name. It was a girl I'd never seen before.

Correction, it was a girl I'd seen before and thought was a guy friend of my brother's. They'd been playing video games in the den since Mom had moved them out of the living room to give me study space for my tutoring sessions with Samuel.

Great. Mom is losing it, and so am I. I'd been a little busy, and having Dorklock out of my biz was such a wonderful thing that I didn't notice for almost two weeks that the kid from school who'd started popping in to play videos with my brother was, in actuality, a girl.

To be fair, she wore a baseball cap, jeans that were more jockey than Juicy, and sweatshirts so big that any budding figure she might be developing was well hidden.

I'm a little ashamed to admit I didn't clue in until the kid stood there in the kitchen, smiling at me as if I were holding the answer to the secret of everything in the universe—maybe even beyond. "Pru?"

I don't know what it was that had made me realize, this time, that she was a girl. Sure, her voice was high like a girl's, but at thirteen, that doesn't mean a thing.

"Yes?" I knew then. Clue #1? None of Dorklock's friends

had ever said a word to me before, not even when we lived in Beverly Hills. And none of them had ever looked with unrequited adoration at the red and green Christmas pom-pom cookies I had made.

After that, everything tumbled into place in a flash. The Dorklock had a girlfriend. Sure, she was skinny and liked video games as much as he did. But she was a girl, and she hung around with him all the time, so, technically, she was a girlfriend.

Which was why I was a little slow to respond when she said, "Can you tell me what to do to make the cheerleading team at Agatha's next year?"

I'd gotten distracted by the whole "Dorklock has a girlfriend and will be going to Agatha's next year" psychic screaming loop.

"Sure." It's not like I hadn't been asked this question before. True, the other times it had been mortals talking to a member of the champion Bevery Hills team. But the answer is the same: "Practice, work hard, and smile."

She had the smile-part down, judging by the sunbeam she shot at me. "I will."

Dorklock sounded annoyed, although he didn't bother to get up from the couch in the den; he just sent his voice into the kitchen. "Pru, stop interrupting our game."

"Get real, you waste of oxygen. She asked me a question and I answered it."

"I'm gonna die here, Hannah, if you don't ignore my sister like she deserves."

Hannah's sunbeam smile disappeared and she popped back, controller in hand, to rescue my brother from whatever monster, menace, or CGI-boogeyman was after him.

Even though I think she has a crush on me. Or sees me as her shortcut to kewl through the secrets of cheerleading.

Too bad she likes bad haircuts, baggy sweatshirts, and video games.

Not to mention the Dorklock. Whom she calls Tobias, with a little sigh on the last syllable. Gag me.

Chapter 11

Mom still hadn't come back, but life had to go on. To-Do was insistent that I get my homework done. I tried to concentrate, but every sound—and our creaky old house makes a ton of creaks, groans, and sighs—made me wonder if Mom had returned. And what she would have to say when she did show up.

Sassy was being a true noodge while I was working on my transubstantion homework. Every time I got close to the end of my incantation, she pounced. Cute, she is, but her claws and kitten teeth still drew blood from my big toe—and threw off my magic big-time.

Finally, I picked her up and brought her eye-to-eye. "What is wrong, Sassy? You have a full food dish and plenty of water. What else does a kitten need?"

She looked at me and yowled. Only this yowl sounded like "witches' council." It did, no matter how impossible that sounds. And just when I was starting to get a clue—accompanied by a sinking feeling in my stomach—she climbed up my arm and latched on to my ear. Before I could say ouch, we weren't in my room anymore.

The first person I noticed was Agatha. The frost white she favored stood out at the council table.

The second person I noticed was Mom, who was standing beside me, looking very unhappy. She had a book in one hand that had a gold title embossed on the dark black leather: *Loss Prevention for Witches*.

It hit me that I'd been summoned to the witches' council. I adjusted quickly, putting a competition smile on my face and dropping my hands so that Sassy sat on my shoulder nibbling on my ear without interference.

I had forgotten that Sassy, the kitten I was given as a familiar for my sweet sixteen birthday party, was supposed to be a conduit to the witches' council. Traitor. I always fed her canned food. But the whole ear-biting transportation-to-the-witches'-council-without-warning thing made me wonder if I ought to switch her to dry.

Whenever I heard anyone talk about the witches' council, I pictured everyone being like Agatha: old, wrinkled, cranky, and all dressed in white. But, as it happened, Agatha was the only one who favored white. The rest were dressed in . . . their own uniquely individual style. One wore an elaborate sari, and one an elegant kimono; one old guy had a kilt on, and one was into red in the same way Agatha was into white. They were all old. And, judging by the way they were looking at me, as cranky as Agatha. Possibly even crankier, although I would have thought that was impossible.

"You have been called to testify in front of the council. Do you swear to tell the truth?"

"Yes." I didn't see that I had any choice. Rumor had it that the council could employ truth spells, potions, and charms until their victims were permanently incapable of telling a lie. Not something most witches were eager to risk. Especially those of us with a year left in high school.

I stood in a penned-in area with two other people. One of them was my mom, and one was someone I'd never seen before. She was beautiful. Probably a Water Talent, by the way she favored blue, kind of foamy clothes. Not that that was always a clue, but with the Water Talents, it usually worked.

"Hi," I whispered to Mom, who I saw now was looking unhappy because I'd been summoned, not because of the whole being-surrounded-by-cranky-ancient-witches thing. "Do you know what's going on?" I pointed my right index finger at the council and my left index finger at the semi-circle of bleachers behind us that held people who were watching everything avidly, though silently. Probably the council had magic-damped them to keep the already cranky council members from going into cranky overload, I guessed.

Mom only had a chance to say, "There's a hearing–" before some big guy with a scythe shouted, "Quiet in the council!"

When a big guy with a scythe asks you to be quiet, you don't argue.

The guy indicated with his scythe that the lady I didn't know should step forward. When she did, a big light surrounded her. Not blinding, but believe me when I say every pore was visible. The judges were going to be able to observe and analyze every muscle twitch and bead of sweat. If she was lying, I had the sinking feeling that they were going to start flinging spells and charms and potions to get the truth out of her.

Old Lady in Red rose into the air and began to glow. I guess she was the boss. "Why did you give birth to your son in the mortal realm?"

Son. Okay. I was off the hook on that one. Unless there was something Mom and Dad hadn't told me? I checked Mom out. She looked worried, but not about me–about the lady being questioned in the harsh light of the council.

"I had no choice. I had only planned to swoop in quickly to hear a performance of the Boston Pops. But before the concert was over, I went into labor and–and the mortals nearby took me to the hospital."

Old Lady in Red frowned and shook her head. Clearly, she didn't like the answer, which seemed pretty simple to me. "How could you have risked going into labor in the mortal realm?"

I tried to witch-whisper to my mom, but I guess the court had spells against it, because all I got was an echo in my ear, "Action forbidden." Too bad. I really wanted to know what was so bad about mortal hospitals. Dorklock and I had been born in one.

I relaxed, though. This had nothing to do with cheerleading. Nothing to do with Agatha's. As far as I could see, this wasn't about me.

Agatha looked at me for a second before she bent forward and asked a question of the shaking witch (you could see her hair vibrating in the light). I hoped she hadn't heard my thoughts.

"Why did you not have a companion to guard you during labor?" she asked.

Guard her? From what? Poor lady. I'd seen one of those birth shows once on TV when I was home from school and too sick to change the channel. It wasn't easy, but the doctors and nurses seemed to know what they're doing.

The poor witch on trial cried even harder. "A friend had planned to go with me, but she heard the northern lights were going to be spectacular over Greenland and decided to go watch them instead at the last minute."

"You should have gone with her."

"I didn't expect to go into labor. It was horrible." She had gone beyond faint trembling to full-scale shaking now. "You don't know how it felt to be whisked away in an ambulance, into a delivery room, and not be able to do anything about it."

"No, I don't." The Old Lady in Red didn't seem all that sympathetic. "That's why witches who could go into labor are advised not to go into the mortal realm. I followed that advice when I gave birth."

Oh. Well. I glanced at Mom. I guess her case was different, since she'd had Dad to watch over us, and had been living in the mortal world.

"I wish I never had. But I didn't think—"

"No." Agatha broke in to the questioning. She sighed like she did with errant students at school. "Your kind never do."

Old Lady in Red asked, "Was the infant ever out of your sight?"

Again, she cried so hard, it seemed like she was going to turn into a puddle of tears. "They took him to the nursery. But as soon as my powers came back the next morning, I asked for him and popped us out of there."

Agatha's next question was asked very quietly, as if she was hoping that that way, she wouldn't get the answer she feared. "So the boy was out of your sight and care overnight?"

"Yes." Tears were running down the witch's cheeks.

There was a moment of silence, and then the light switched off.

I thought I'd be popped back home with Mom, but instead I stood in the dark, listening to the sound of what seemed like wings flapping in the breeze. I hoped it wasn't the flying monkeys, the ones that came after Daniel and me after we'd been caught kissing in the time bubble.

When the light blasted back on, I closed my eyes for a second. I opened them, slightly teary from the assault of the spotlights, to see Angelo in front of the witches' council. The light was focused on him. Even in that nasty, unforgiving light, he was a perfect 10. The council members made startled little sounds. I could see the observers behind me lean forward, even though I couldn't hear the sounds they made. Sighs, probably.

He blinked. Then he blinked again and rubbed his eyes. I realized that he thought he was dreaming. Boy, was he in for a surprise.

Before I could be told it was against the rules, I waved at him. "Welcome to witch world, Angelo." I tried to see the witch part of him, but all I saw was the same old hotness as always. Was he really a witch switched at birth with a mortal boy?

"Pru?" He did a double take, then gave me a faint wave back.

The Old Lady in Red commanded, "Examine him!"

A wizened old witch floated over to Angelo and placed his hands on Angelo's cheeks. He bent his head close to Angelo's. He took a deep breath and held it for moment. Then he let it out in a rush and he turned to the council. "This boy is indeed a witch. I can sense his Talent is strong. I suspect Patience Stewart is correct, and he has manifested an Attractivity Talent while living in the wild with mortals."

Angelo had a *Talent*? I was bumming now. How come he didn't even know he was a witch and his Talent showed up, anyway? I wouldn't exactly call that fair. Of course, it was interesting that Angelo was a witch. That meant he was no longer off-limits as potential boyfriend material. Didn't it? As long as I left Tara out of the equation.

"I think there's been a mistake," Angelo said calmly, addressing the council as if he were in his own house instead of in front of a council of scary-looking witches. He looked at each one of them and smiled.

"Maybe there has been," Agatha said soothingly.

I thought she was joking. Until I looked at her face and realized that her wrinkles could not obscure a definite effort to flirt with Angelo—a boy the same age as her great-grandson to the nth, Daniel!

Even the witches on the council weren't immune to his charm. Kilt guy said a hasty spell to dampen Angelo's Talent, and Agatha—and all the female witches on the council—sighed and shook themselves a bit before continuing. They asked him things they already knew, like his age and name and where he was born. He answered, though I think there may have been a spell compelling him to, given his scowl. Even I could see he was the son of the first witch I'd seen being questioned. There was a very strong resemblance between them.

The questioning was not the most productive. It seemed like they already knew all the answers and were just going through the formalities for some reason. Maybe to give Angelo time to get used to the idea that he was a witch. Angelo hadn't believed in witches ten seconds before he was popped into this room to answer questions about his birth—questions that were asked by people even he couldn't doubt were actual witches. He was taking the knowledge that he was a witch pretty well. Or maybe he was just in denial.

The council didn't seem worried about whether he was happy about finding out he was a witch. Right after they stopped lobbing questions at him, they started lobbing rules. The rules they set on him were pretty harsh. He couldn't tell his mortal parents that he was a witch. He must leave their home at eighteen and never talk to them again. He couldn't see his real parents until he'd been properly educated and evaluated and everyone had signed off that he was a witch without any glitches from being raised by mortals for so long. His Talent would be bound until the final decision too. He'd learn to use it in controlled situations only. I took that to mean among men, since his Talent unbound pretty much seemed to devastate women.

After rattling off these rules, Agatha then asked, "Do you understand you must abide by these rules and begin your witch training without delay?"

I remember how Angelo had always said he didn't feel like he belonged. He'd straightened, and stopped shaking his head about halfway through the questioning. It didn't surprise me at all when he said, "I do," without hesitation.

He was just that kind of guy, whether he was a mortal or a witch.

"We will let you know of our decision to accept you as a lost witch after we have finished with our testimony," Agatha said.

The guy with the scythe pointed at Angelo, and he disappeared. Then the scythe pointed at my mom, and suddenly she was in the light. I was surprised to see what good pores she had.

"We have reviewed your evidence that this boy, born of a witch, switched with a mortal at birth, is indeed a witch. We concur."

Agatha leaned forward. "How did you come by this evidence?"

Mom didn't seem all that nervous in front of the council. "My daughter made friends with the boy, and I had the opportunity to observe his ability to attract the attention of females of all ages."

Agatha, of course, leaned forward. "Including yourself?"

Mom glanced at me guiltily, then nodded. "Including myself. The boy's Talent will be a strong one, and I recognized immediately that he needs someone to teach him to control it. Prudence can testify that I did not waste time in informing the council as soon as I realized what must have happened. I knew he needed immediate intervention."

"It may be too late for re-education," Agatha said in her typical glum way. "Stronger measures may be called for."

Okay. I'm not a dummy, but this was my first visit to the council and the whole thing was throwing me off my game. Stronger measures didn't sound good, but I didn't really clue until the light was on me.

"Prudence Stewart, it is our understanding that you know the boy who was switched at birth. Is that correct?"

"I know him." I didn't like her tone, so I said a little tartly, "His name is Angelo."

The lady next to me—Angelo's mother—cried harder.

I added, "But he's not a witch, he's a mortal." Weird that I was fighting for Angelo to be mortal, since that made him off-limits again. I just couldn't believe it—it was all happening so quickly.

"Do you presume to tell the council that you do not believe in DNA tests?"

"No!" I floundered. "But . . . but . . . he can't summon. I've never seen him even try to cast a spell."

"You have not felt the pull of his Attractivity Talent?" Agatha looked at me with narrowed eyes that make more wrinkles in her face. I knew she was thinking of Daniel. She'd always blamed me. Said I was a bad influence, even though everyone said Daniel had been incorrigible before I came onto the scene.

Oh. Well, then. "I meant, I didn't know he was a witch. I thought he was a mortal."

"So you have not observed him doing magic, even unintentionally? Say, summoning something to eat when he is very hungry?"

"No." Was that good or bad? I couldn't tell. "Maybe."

"Make up your mind, girl." This time, it was Old Lady in Red who was impatient with me.

"I didn't think of it as magic before, just some serious chemistry. But if he is a witch, then I think maybe he can make girls like him a lot."

"The Attractivity Talent." Agatha nodded. Then she shook her head gravely. "One of the most dangerous of the Fire Talents for the untrained."

"But he's not a hound at all," I protested. It sounded like Angelo needed protecting. "He doesn't take advantage. He doesn't even seem to know why all the girls like him so much."

That didn't make the council members any happier.

The light switched off me and back to the lady next to me. Angelo's mother looked utterly miserable. I checked her out more closely. She did have those nice lips like his. Her eyes were blue, but her dark lashes were long, like his. Even though the evidence was pretty clear, the whole thing was still hard to believe.

The one slightly positive thing about the whole experience was that, despite all of Agatha's huffing and puffing, she wasn't trying to blow down the house of Pru. Not today, anyway.

Just when I started to relax, the light spotlighted me again. The Old Lady in Red looked at me, and she was scarier than Agatha. "Have you any reason to feel magicked upon when you are in your home?"

"No." Magicked upon? Even the Dorklock wouldn't dare cast a spell on me with Mom on eagle-eye watch. But then I realized she was asking about Angelo again. The light went off of me and onto Angelo's mom again.

"Celestial Fleur, do you relinquish all responsibility for the education and testing of your son, the mortal-raised boy Angelo, should the council decide to grant him a probationary testing period to see if the damage done to him during his formative years can be reversed?"

If? I wondered what the alternative would be, but with Agatha and the Old Lady in Red in charge, I couldn't imagine Angelo would enjoy it.

"I could see to his education myself," Angelo's birth mom said. But even I knew, given her Water Talent ethereal nature, that that was not a good idea. I would have to remember to ask Mom how a Water Talent could give birth to a Fire Talent. I watched her pat Celestial Fleur's arm soothingly. Mom was an Air Talent, and Dorklock had a Magic Talent. I wonder what my Talent would be—if I ever manifested one.

"That is not wise. You have done enough for him," the Old Lady in Red said dryly. "You must relinquish all responsibility for his education and agree not to contact him until he is rehabilitated and has proven himself a true witch."

More tears. But she was brave enough to say through them, "I will."

"The council will inform you of their decision shortly."

Old Lady in Red didn't bother with unsilencing the gallery crowd; she just waved them away. Back to whatever they had been doing, I presumed, but I spent the next few moments of silence wondering about it. Wondering about what was going to happen to Angelo was way too scary.

"We'll take your evidence under advisement and let you know our decision posthaste," Agatha told mom and me.

We were back in the kitchen before the words had finished echoing around the council chamber.

Sassy leaped into my lap as I sat there, staring at Mom, speechless, clueless, and wondering if I'd dreamed the whole thing. Mom was looking at me with a look that said something big had gone down.

"What just happened?" I asked her.

She didn't let me get away with pretending I hadn't understood. "You were there."

"So Angelo was switched at birth? That's not his fault. The council can't—"

She rubbed her temples. "They can, but I think they'll give him a chance. He hasn't caused any magic trouble. And Celestial didn't realize how close to giving birth she was when she went to that concert."

I thought about what I'd heard in the council. "Which meant she brought a mortal kid home with her. What happened to him?"

Mom tapped the book she'd been holding during the session. "When it was clear he was mortal, he was put up for adoption through the Great Wings adoption service."

Wasn't that kind of harsh? "You make it sound routine."

"Sometimes a witch gives birth to a child who does not have the ability to perform magic, Pru. It isn't unheard of. Although I would have thought Celestial might have realized that there might be a bigger problem when her son showed no sign of magic development. But there is no love as blind as a mother's love."

I thought of Mrs. Kenton. Angelo's mom, I'd thought, until now. "Mrs. Kenton will freak."

Mom shook her head. "Fortunately, she'll never know."

"But if Angelo—"

"I've already suggested a plan to the council. If they agree with it, Angelo will live with the Kentons while he's being schooled in magic. Mrs. Kenton will never know."

"What if Angelo slips?" It wasn't easy for me to live in witch world, and I had always known I was a witch.

"Pru, this isn't the first time such a thing has happened. Witches lose their powers briefly after they give birth, and labor is not something you can schedule in your planner— not even as fancy a planner as To-Do."

"Wow. I'm surprised you would have me and Dorklock in the hospital, then."

Mom smiled. "That was different. Grandmama was there to put a charm on you so that you could not be taken far from me." She shook her head sadly. "Poor Celestial, she's in such pain. But as long as Angelo becomes a true witch, she can make up for lost time with him for many centuries."

"If not?" I wasn't really sure I wanted the answer to that question, but I had to ask.

"In the past, when the council decided to try to bring a lost child back into the witch realm, many protective spells have been cast to keep the mortal realm unaware."

"And when they didn't work?"

"I don't think we need to worry about that." Mom didn't look at me. "There have only been a few cases where a lost child has had his magic curdle inside and release evil forces that can't be contained. Like with Jack the Ripper."

"Jack the Ripper was a witch?" No wonder the council members looked like they wanted to shake Celestial Fleur until her teeth knocked together.

"A lost witch. He was much too old by the time we realized. He had to be—" She stopped. "Well, never mind. You and I both realize that Angelo is one of the kindest boys you know, human or mortal."

True enough. So why were the hairs on the back of my neck standing on end?

Chapter 12

I can't tell you how weird it was when Angelo showed up to "car pool" with me to school. Really. Somehow the witches' council had made Mrs. Kenton believe that she had filled in the application and visited Agatha's to get Angelo accepted. Mom was on deck for car-pool duty, or so Mrs. Kenton thought.

She showed up with Angelo the first day, which was no surprise at all. "I'm so grateful that you helped Angelo get into Agatha's," she gushed to Mom. "It's such a wonderful school. He'll have no trouble getting into any of the Ivy Leagues now." She beamed as she stood there in the living room.

Mom was having a little trouble figuring out how to get rid

of her when Mrs. Kenton glanced out to the driveway and said, "I have no trouble taking my turn at car pool, either."

Oh. Car pool meant sharing the driving. Apparently, Mom saw the problem at the same moment I did, and she had an answer ready. "I'm working at the school, so I have to go every day, anyway. It's no trouble to add an extra person to the commute." The commute. Cute, Mom.

Mrs. Kenton was not to be budged, however, until Mom, Angelo, Dorklock, and I climbed into my little Jetta (which I've been neglecting for studying, practice, and extra-credit projects) and drove away. She stood at the curb and waved until we were out of sight. At which point, Mom pulled over to the curb and then popped us back to garage.

Angelo looked a little shell-shocked. I smiled at him in sympathy. At least I'd known I was a witch when I started school at Agatha's. "We don't drive to Agatha's. We pop."

He shrugged. "When in Rome . . . build a coliseum. Right?" He smiled and I noticed, really noticed, that the warm buzz I usually got being near Angelo was gone. His smile actually gave me a slightly negative reaction, as if I'd caught sight of a piece of spinach stuck between his teeth. The council's spell had seriously bound his Talent. I didn't want to be shallow, though, so I made myself remember how nice Angelo had always been to me.

"Right." I took his hand and popped us both to the school office. "You're going to learn to do that soon, and once you're in school, they take care of all the popping." I moved aside to let the school secretary welcome Angelo like she had me—with a cold finger on his forehead.

He looked at me a little nervously. "That finger just put your whole schedule on record. You'll be automatically popped to classes, to the main hallway so you can use your locker, and to lunch. Handy, huh?"

One day I'd have to tell him how lucky he was to have me escort him to the office. When your magic is shaky, you can mis-pop and embarrass yourself horribly. Like I did my first day at Agatha's when I mis-popped into the broom closet of the boy's locker room, where I had a view of Mr. Bindlebrot (math teacher/Dragon Ball coach) in a towel. Somehow, though, I don't think Angelo is ready to appreciate how lucky he has it here. Yet.

"Sure." By the time Angelo had replied to my comment, we'd been popped into the main hall with our lockers.

Tara was standing next to my locker, the fateful number 666 that had given Daniel the nickname he used for me when I first came to school. "Angelo! Pru told me you'd be here this morning."

Angelo lifted his hand in a weak wave. "Hi, Tara. This is some school you've got here."

"Yeah." She looked at him, smiled in sympathy, and then slowly stopped. "What happened to you?"

"I just found out I was a witch. Isn't that enough?" He

seemed a little annoyed at the way she was staring at him like he was a stranger.

I witch-whispered to Tara, "He has binding spells on his Talent, for obvious reasons. I *told* you that." Not that I had understood how different Angelo would seem with the binding spells in place.

"Oh." She smiled at him. She was so over him, it showed from her head to her toes. "Good luck with that."

The bell rang, a familiar sound to anyone who has been to school, mortal or witch. Before I could explain the drill, Angelo disappeared to his first class, probably remedial magic with Mr. Phogg, if his schedule was anything like mine was when I came to Agatha's. I hoped he didn't hate the remedial classes as much as I had.

I took To-Do out of my pocket. "Add action item: Help Angelo get into regular magic classes ASAP."

Instead of being popped into my first class, I ended up in the gym. I thought it was a mistake until I saw that the rest of the squad was there, along with our coach. And then my stomach started doing dive rolls. Coach Gertie looked grim. Which, on a normal scale of grimness was about a 5, but for Coach Gertie a 5 was off the scale. She didn't even try for a smile. Her hair, which was a bird's nest normally, looked like the birds had had a big fight.

"Girls, I'm afraid we're not going to be able to compete

in the National Competition. In fact, I'm afraid our awards ceremony is cancelled. As is our cheering at the magic game on Friday."

"What?" We practically cheered the question, with pom-poms raised. We were all on the same page, it seemed—the outraged page. "Why can't we cheer at the magic game?"

Coach Gertie shook her head and lifted her arms in the air. Our angry babble silenced—our mouths were moving, but the sound had been banished to some other dimension.

"The magic game is a one-time ban." Coach Gertie frowned. "There's been some concern that the"—she glanced at me and then looked away quickly—"disruptions we've experienced the first part of the year need to be straightened out. Therefore, our headmistress has put a moratorium on all things mortal."

"All things mortal?" The other girls looked at me. Charity was the only one who smiled. The rest of them looked mega unhappy. I decided to take it as a sign that my life was not over. Yet.

"*All* things," I said slowly. Coach Gertie didn't look at me.

"Why? Is it because of the bruises—or is it that new guy, Angelo? It's not our fault he got switched at birth." Elektra had jumped to the wrong conclusion, but I didn't imagine it would take too long before the whole school knew the truth. The new mortal ban was due to me, Prudence Stewart. Like it was my fault that my family had moved next door to a witch switched at birth with a mortal. Sigh. I didn't think it was going to be a popularity booster.

"Of course it's not the squad's fault." Coach Gertie shook her head and raised her whistle, but didn't blow it. "Things like this happen when we're not careful about how we proceed in the mortal realm. We don't want to take it for granted. We don't want to forget how dangerous it can be. Do we?"

"Competing's not dangerous," Tara argued with the exact words I was too afraid to say with the mortal bull's-eye Agatha had painted on my forehead. "None of us are going to accidentally get lost in the mortal realm. We know what we're doing. We'll be careful."

There was a wail from meek little Sunita. "If we don't compete, we'll be losers." Who knew she had such a competitive streak?

"Nonsense." Coach Gertie frowned more deeply. "That's the kind of thinking that Agatha is worried about. That's mortal talk—losers, winners. Those are the concepts of short life spans and limited magic ability."

Sure, it was. Tell that to my grandfather—who enjoyed "playing" in Vegas, and definitely wanted to win, not lose, at the poker table.

"We've done all the hard work." Elektra wasn't buying the witch party line. "Never mind being losers. We won't get a chance to prove to ourselves that we've improved ourselves."

"That's simply not true." Coach Gertie was trying to sound reassuring, but she couldn't put out a raging inferno with a cup of white lies. "Your work in magic cheering has been greatly improved by your work at mortal routines. You will reap the benefits at every magic game."

Tara asked the next logical question. "Does that mean we can't play mortal teams anymore? What about the football team?"

Coach Gertie looked troubled. "Agatha has said so, but we coaches are not happy. We are appealing the ruling. Agatha has granted permission for the football team to play in this weekend's game, but without cheerleaders."

Tara was shocked enough that she practically whispered, "So sports can compete, but cheerleaders can't even cheer, never mind compete?"

"Unfair," we all murmured.

Coach Gertie shrugged. "Sports are—"

"More important," we all finished for her. It wasn't like we hadn't heard it before.

"Girls!" Coach Gertie was not happy. But she was the kind of grown-up unhappy that meant she wasn't going to make a fuss. Witch grown-ups stick together just like mortal adults do, I guess.

"Agatha has spoken. I'll hear no more." Coach Gertie put another silencing spell on us. We waved our arms in protest, but she was not going to give in. Instead, she crossed her arms and stood tapping her toe, waiting for us to stop protesting.

What signs was she looking for, since she couldn't hear a word out of our mouths? Well, after we stopped flapping our gums, hopping up and down, and crying—basically stopped everything except breathing and blinking—she lifted the binding spell.

We just stood there, stunned into silence. Stunned into a place cheerleaders fear to tread: the no-compete zone. I mean, sure, cheerleaders are there to get the crowd on the team's side, to cheer the team on and all. But let's get real. What we most want to do is make the other team's cheerleaders look clueless, uncoordinated, and apathetic. I mean, really, why else do we polish our routines and risk our necks if it isn't to have the crowd think we are the best cheerleaders ever to cheer? I was deeply disappointed in Coach Gertie for not understanding that.

If you've never been in a room full of teenage girls when they're all upset, you may not understand the way the atmosphere gets heavy and crackly at the same time. In a room full of teenage witches? Umm. Let's just say that anything not nailed down got caught up in a whirlwind and turned into confetti.

The mutual temper tantrum lasted about sixty seconds. And then we stopped—in synch. We restored everything and went back to our regularly scheduled classes without protest. Anyone watching might have thought we had accepted the inevitable. Hah! Agatha had created a monster, and I don't think she had a clue.

I hadn't expected to get much sympathy from the fringie side of the fence when I stopped by their table at lunch to explain that Agatha had finally found a way to really punish me for Daniel having run away from school. After all, no one expected her to be fair, or even reasonable. That would be like Milan haute couture models suddenly having healthy appetites.

But I was pleased to see that they got why it *was* unfair. So many people don't understand that cheering is hard work, not just shaking a little pom-pom at the crowd. Samuel even suggested we stage a sit-in.

"Sure. A sit-in. For witches?" I tried to picture it, but the mind-film stopped short at witches ever doing anything together. Not to mention that the only student I knew who was willing (and able) to break the school rules at will had been Daniel. "This school is so spelled and charmed to keep us from doing much more than breathe, you really think we could carry out a sit-in without Agatha blowing us out of her hair with one frigid breath?"

It was Denise who broke the awkward silence by commenting, "You don't sound like you, Pru. Where's the insane optimism you usually show?"

"Everything I'm trying to do is falling apart. The head-mistress thinks I'm infecting her school with mortal cooties. I almost failed math—which used to be my best subject. I'm just barely unsuspended from my cheerleading team. And now we can't cheer in mortal games—or compete."

Samuel looked at me seriously. "If you were suspended from your team, and you couldn't play, would you still fight for the cheerleaders to be able to cheer?"

"Of course." Because he was my friend, and a clueless fringie, I tried to keep too much "duh" out of my tone.

Denise shook her head. "Such dedication over something so superficial."

Okay. So I *thought* she got it, but I was wrong. "Since when is supporting, encouraging, and rallying around your team a superficial thing?" I really hate it when people, even my friends, diss cheerleading. "Do you know how hard it is to keep your spirits up when your team is losing fifty to two? And the quarterback is a butterfingers?"

They looked at me blankly. None of them were sports fans. "Okay, how annoying has it been for you to support me in sitting at that cheerleading table? Annoyance factor of ten, right? But you understood why I needed to bond with my team. You understood it was important to me. And you were there for me. So who's superficial now?"

I stalked off to the cheer table without another word.

Never underestimate the power of an annoyed fringie.

Or a good sit-in (picture witches hovering midair, though, not grubbing on the ground—oh, and no long hair or bell-bottoms).

Apparently, my friends knew how to come through big-time. At first it was a little trickle—Maria at the jocks table, whispering until they were frowning. Denise over with the black-loving/death-worshipping crowd, making them breathe hard enough that they got color in their normally pale cheeks. And Samuel. Samuel had saved the best group for himself: the science, math, and all-around geeks.

It was the geeks who made the sit-in possible, of course. They were the ones who countered the school spells that would normally send us to our classes automatically. The counterspells would keep us all sitting in our places when the bell sounded—the bell that normally sent us back to the hallway with our lockers, and the second bell that sent us back to classes.

The goths took the protest to another level. They understood that it wasn't enough to just sit in the lunchroom. They had a handle on the importance of presentation. Hence the floating-in-air thing, and the glowing, hovering protest signs done in our school colors of black, orange, and red—a red the color of fresh, dripping blood.

Agatha's decision had made the square pegs decide to drum their edges against the round holes. It was amazing to see the protest come together with whispers and questioning glances that quickly turned into motion and sound and light. The scariest thing was that everyone was looking at me—even Tara.

"We're not being unreasonable." I spun in a slow circle so that I could address everyone in the room. If I learned anything growing up in Beverly Hills, it was that you had to take advantage of the spotlight while it was still on you. "We deserve our chance to do what we do best, to do what we love. We're not hurting anyone. Right?"

"Yeah!" Even the jocks agreed, although I couldn't help but be suspicious that they were only in it for the time-off-for-bad-behavior perk.

When the bell sounded—the one that usually had us heading toward our lockers before the second bell, which popped us all automatically to our classes—I held my breath. No one moved. We all looked at one another, and then we grinned. Totally kewl. Until Agatha—probably alerted by school alarms—popped in, trailed by a swirl of white mist.

"I will expel anyone still in this lunchroom when the second bell sounds." She lifted her left fist into the air, pointing toward the double doors that led out to our hall lockers.

The bell sounded. I'm sure some people disappeared, but so few that I couldn't tell who might have been afraid of Agatha's true wrath.

I remembered getting caught in the time bubble with

Daniel, and the screeching monkeys that came after us to expel us from school. Would Agatha unleash those monkeys on a lunchroom full of students?

But Agatha had a threat bigger than expelling us up her long white sleeve. Of course.

When no one moved as the bell rang, she narrowed her eyes and swiveled her head around, to make sure she made eye contact with every single one of us. "Very well," she said, much too quietly for my liking. I'd expected her to be breathing fire by now.

But she didn't breathe fire. She just lifted both hands in the air, closed her eyes, and summoned our parents. All of them. And she silenced with a lift of her finger all the questions and complaints that naturally arose from witches disturbed in the middle of their daily routines.

Agatha was a powerful witch, but I'd never really understood how powerful until that moment. There is something quite terrifying about a single, white-clad, wrinkled woman who can shut up a room full of angry adult witches with one twitch of her finger. So why, all of a sudden, did I think, I want to be like her someday?

I quickly squashed the thought, but it was the kind that had a life of its own. No doubt I'd dream of it—and have nightmares, too—until I was as powerful as Agatha. Of course, I'd avoid the white—and the wrinkles, too.

"Your children have defied the school rules to protest my

ban on fraternizing with mortals. Are you going to do something about this, or should I?" She wagged her finger, and the parents were once again able to speak.

"The mortal realm is not a playground for the bored witch." One apoplectic dad shook his finger in the air as he roared at us.

Okay, that was just a lie. Grandmama showed me that when I was just a kid. She loved the mortal gadgets—she even had a car that she enjoyed driving around every now and then. Not that I could say that to parents. For some reason, kids—this applies to witches and to mortal kids alike—are not supposed to make the same mistakes, have the same urges, or do the same things that our parents did.

What's even sillier is that *our* parents already went through this with *their* parents and they *still* don't get it. Sigh. But that's not my battle today.

I floated into the air and created a light glow around the edges of my hair. A very kewl effect for cheerleading, but versatile enough for getting the attention of a maddened crowd, too. "We just want you to listen to us," I said, speaking softly so as not to offend those parents who consider anything beyond a polite whisper to be youthful belligerence. I did make sure my whisper carried equally to every part of the room. A message isn't effective if it can't be heard.

I didn't wait for the room to get completely quiet. I don't

think a room full of angry parents is ever completely quiet. "All we're asking for is a chance to show how good we are at competition. If we had our own competitions, we wouldn't need to compete with mortals. But we don't. And so we have to follow mortal rules and risk a few bumps and bruises. Is that really so bad?"

An anxious mother—one of those Water Talent types who is all floaty and teary—shook her head. "You don't know what you're getting into. There are so many temptations in the mortal realm: You could get addicted to cheating at mortal competitions and find yourselves on the wrong side of the witches' council's laws for fair contact. Do you know the penalty for breaking those laws?"

Agatha's eyes practically glowed at the opportunity to point out my ignorance. "Miss Stewart has, unfortunately, been raised in the mortal world for most of her life. She is not aware of most of the laws and their consequences, except for the ones she has already broken."

The parents all got looks that ranged between horrified and nauseated at the idea that their children may have been exposed to my mortal cooties.

I knew I had to do some major mercy-of-the-court work ASAP. "I'm a little behind on the witches' council's laws," I admitted. "But I know competition and I know cheering. Not to mention what we've gotten from setting a goal to compete in mortal competition: better routines, better skills, better timing, and a way to push ourselves to be the best we can be. I thought witch parents wanted that for their children too?"

One of the more reasonable parents shouted, "Maybe we should begin a witch cheerleading competition!"

"Maybe." It was time to play hardball. "And maybe we should start a witch-only football competition."

"That's a bit drastic, don't you think?" That, from the father of our best linebacker.

Umm, yeah, that's the point. Not that I was going to say so out loud. I just asked innocently, "Why? If we can't compete against mortals, why can the football team? Or the baseball team? Or the swimming team?"

"Or track?" someone called out from the jock crowd.

I smiled, ready to go on forever, until I got down to the chess club and the bowling league and the debate team. "Or–"

"Enough!" Agatha raised herself to my level and totally stole my light-outlining idea. Only she didn't stop at the hair, but outlined all of herself so she glowed like a radioactive snow witch. "We are not here to discuss any current school programs or policies. We are here to discuss student misbehavior."

Tara floated up beside me, pom-poms in her hand. She was wearing her uniform. "We aren't misbehaving. We're just trying to get your attention so we can be like every other team in the school and get a chance to compete fairly."

"Do you know how many rules you are breaking?" Agatha demanded.

"Five," Denise answered as she floated up beside me. "One, casting unauthorized spells in school. Two, failure to go to class. Three, wasting the headmistress's time. Four, refusing to obey a direct order by a teacher or headmistress. And five, disrupting the school day." She smiled. "I don't think I missed any, did I?"

Agatha gaped for a second before she exploded. "Insolence!" Way to go, Denise!

Maria looked positively angelic when she floated up, her short, curly hair haloing around her face like a . . . well, like a halo. "I don't think insolence is explicitly against the rules, though I believe it is implied in both the rule against disobeying a teacher and the rule against cutting class."

I wondered if Agatha could hate me more, but I didn't have time to worry about that. "Look." I made my head glow blue, just to stand out in the now-glowing group floating around me. "All we want is a chance to cheer as much as we can—and also to get better by competing against other great teams in the regional and national competitions. What's so wrong with that?"

The Water Talent mom had stopped crying, but still had some worries. "Why can't you just enjoy cheering like witches? Why take the risk of cheering like mortals?"

It was a fair question—not to mention a great sign that

some of the parents were listening. "It's hard to explain. But, if Agatha will let us cheer at the Dragon Ball game on Friday night, we can show you what practicing and competing has done for us so far. I think you'd be impressed. That's all we're asking. Then, if we haven't done a great job, we'll stop competing. If we have, you'll let us compete."

They still didn't look happy, so I added, "And we'll start trying to organize a witches-only cheerleading competition for next year. Okay?"

"I think that's fair," the football father said. Other parents were nodding and murmuring, probably eager to get this over with and get back to whatever it was they had been doing when Agatha summoned them.

Agatha wasn't happy to have the tide turned from her wrath. But she didn't argue. "We'll see what happens at the Dragon Ball game, then." She wasn't finished. "And detentions for all of you."

I made a counteroffer. "Wouldn't it be better if we earn detentions only if we aren't right to fight for our competition?"

She took a deep breath and stared at me for a long time. "Fine, Miss Stewart. It will make the stakes more interesting. Double the detention if you don't convince us that mortal competition improves your performance at witches-only games."

Great. I always like to say I love a challenge. But did it have to be *double* detention?

On the sunny side, I had managed to convince the parents to let us show them why this mortal training was good for us. How it had helped us to be better cheerleaders, better athletes. I searched through the crowd to see if I could spot Mom, but she was hidden somewhere in the mass of witch parents. Too bad. I would have liked to have known whether she was smiling or frowning. It would have given me a clue as to how unhappy my home life was going to be for the next few weeks.

I didn't really know how I was going to use the magic game routines to underscore that it was practicing like mortals that had given us the edge, but never mind that teensy little detail. I'd come up with something. I was Prutastic, after all.

Not one to like going without a backup plan, I also thought I'd track Daniel, since he might be the only thing standing between Agatha, me, and total meltdown. What a peace offering it would be if I could convince Daniel to come back to school—if I could find him. I'd had success with tracking Samuel. How hard could it be to track down one rebel without an escape clause—just because no one else had been able to do it? Piece of cake. Or maybe tritium.

Chapter 13

The stands were jammed for our Dragon Ball game. It was going to be a night of full-on magic for the Dragon Ball players, the cheerleaders, and the fans in the stands. I still wasn't quite adjusted to the oomph factor that magic brought to the games. Not that it mattered. We were on, and we had to shine. Success meant the difference between our competition hopes and two days of detention. It also meant the chance to show off our stuff in a way we never had before.

Sure, magic cheerleading is pretty amazing, and it was the first time I saw it. But we'd taken it to a new level—cleaned up the sloppy edges and introduced the concept of synchronicity and teamwork that had been missing before.

One thing I'd had to learn the hard way in my early

months at Agatha's: Witches are just a bit independent, and cheerleading witches all like to be center stage. It had taken a bit of getting used to, but I'd managed. And I'd also managed to strike a balance between acting like a team and getting a shot at the center-stage spotlight.

With the nature of witches in mind, not to mention the ability to use magic in our routines, I'd created a routine that had a big start, a huge middle, and a blockbuster ending. If we pulled it off from start to finish, the parents *had* to let us compete. There'd be no way they could say no.

If we didn't pull it off, then we didn't deserve to compete. I'm not sure we'd deserve the detentions, but we'd serve them. Agatha wouldn't have it any other way.

I knew the crowd would go wild when they saw us. Which didn't make me a bit less nervous when we started. No matter how good you know you can be, there's nothing more dangerous than overconfidence the first time you try out a new routine. Or the tenth time you do it, for that matter.

I was definitely not over the confidence line inside, although I was upbeat and positive on the outside. But Tara was on the verge. She'd already decided our new routines were going to be our ticket to running the school.

"Ready?" she asked as she got into place beside me.

"More than ready," I answered.

She saw Angelo giving us the thumbs-up and frowned. "We are so over, but he isn't getting the clue."

"I think he's just being friendly and supportive, Tara. Besides, you know the council cast spells on him up the wazoo so that he doesn't have girls crawling all over him while he's learning to control his magic. It's not that easy to make friends with all that going on. He needs his old friends."

"Whatever. I just wish he'd stop–" She didn't have a word for what she wanted. I think it was probably "living," but I wasn't going to supply it. Tara had been way into the forbidden-fruit angle of Angelo, but I wasn't going to let her abandon him as a friend. To make it at Agatha's, he needed every friend he could get.

I smiled and waved at Angelo, even if the hottie factor had cooled to minus ten. I knew it was only temporary, and I counted on Samuel–with a little help from me–to get him up to speed on the magic so that he could be back to normal by next year. It would be one great senior year if we made it happen.

I liked Angelo. Sure, it was weird that I'd worried about him being a mortal when it turned out he wasn't, but hey, I'd learned to deal with being yanked out of the mortal world into the witch world. I felt for the guy.

Not so Tara. She really didn't like the fact that Angelo had turned out to be a witch. I don't think I needed to worry about being jealous of her any longer. Even if Angelo got his Talent unbound tomorrow, Tara had moved on. In one way, that was good for me since I'd be free to ask him out next year, when the witches' council lifted the binding spells. If I was still interested, of course. But I couldn't worry about that now. The game was about to begin.

Dragon Ball is an interesting game, played by witches for as long as history records. Some even say the game used to be played with dragons. These days it was played on paper dragons, animated only by the power of the witch mounted upon it.

I haven't quite figured out the rules, but basically it involves flying paper dragons, balls of flame, buckets of water, and ten poles covered with pitch on either team's side that must be burned to the ground before the game ends.

Cheering for Dragon Ball is surprisingly easy: Our team on fire, bad; their team on fire, good. Also, get out of the way of both flameballs and waterbuckets, because either can leave you with a bad-hair day.

So we knew we were going to have to put on a really spectacular show if we were competing with the fast-action and dramatic plays of Dragon Ball. Fortunately, we were prepared. We'd already decided that we were going to unveil our new wowalicious routine at this game, but the pressure of knowing how high the stakes were made the adrenaline flow like we were at a competition.

Celestina asked, a little hesitantly—her instincts as a cheerleader were good, but she just couldn't trust herself, or

the team, enough to be as positive as she needed to be—
"What if we blow it?"

I was really going to have to work on this whole spread-ing-the-negative-vibe thing. Team members should prop one another up before a game or a competition—and there should never be negative talk during the game. Sigh.

Oh well, time for a little Pru-attitude-altitude. "We're not going to blow it. We're going to wow our parents like we've never wowed them before."

Charity said, a bit uncharitably, "I don't want to serve double detention."

"Great!" I refused to let my smile drop one megawatt as I faced the crowd. "I don't even want to serve a single deten-tion. I bet no one here does. Am I right?"

We all raised our pom-poms and gave a shout in agree-ment on that one. No-brainer, on my part. Detention at Agatha's involves being immobilized in a quicksand-like substance. Not fun at all. I had to do it once and that was definitely more than enough.

Sunita had a panicked look on her face. "I'm going to for-get that third step-step bit, I know it. And then everything will be off and someone's going to get hurt."

It doesn't take long for panic to become contagious. I had to do something, and I had to do it fast. I witch-whispered in everyone's ear, "Relax, I'll make sure everyone is on task. Your cheer-whisperer is on the job."

I wasn't sure I could do that and keep on task myself with these mega-new routines, but by the look on everyone's face, I realized I had succeeded. Wipe another item off the To-Do list. Soon I wouldn't need the Troll doll, and I wouldn't have to suffer the pinches he liked to give me to keep me on task, either.

Tara smiled. "Good idea, Pru."

And just in time, because our mega-opening started at the moment our Dragon Ball team all got on the field. We had cast spells to cause our hair to rise and move around our faces like flames as we rose into the air and began to cheer for our team to win.

The crowd noticed that we moved together. We noticed we moved together. All I'd had to whisper was, "Up." And then, "Down."

The next wowalicious move was more difficult: a sequence that was carefully timed to the music. I just said, "Back left. Back middle. Back right." It was tricky because I had to time the whisper so they could hear and respond exactly at the right moment in the music. We were amazing, if I do say so myself. And I didn't let myself worry that although the crowd applauded, no one got to their feet and there were no fan bursts of magic confetti.

The most coordinated, and rather impressive, routine we had I'd named the fountain. It was a flying take on the pyramid, with a waterfall twist.

We started on the floor, in a circle, our arms in the air, and smoke flowing like water from our fingertips to our toes. We looked like a ring of water flowing from an unseen source. Not bad for a start, but then we made it better.

As the water illusion took hold, every other member of the circle did a lazy somersault upward, letting the smoke water flow upward, at first, and then, as we formed a second, smaller ring atop the larger circle, back down, like a water fountain. We stayed there a moment, listening to the crowd's hushed murmurs. Come on, people, I silently urged the faces in the stands, *feel* the magic.

And then, once more, half of the second tier of our water fountain divided again and formed a tighter circle above. A three-tiered fountain effect.

This time, the clapping was thunderous. Even though we couldn't see the crowd through the water illusion, we could hear their reaction. The stunt looked way kewl, and I hoped it would be the routine that finally got the parents to see that we had become great cheerleaders by learning a few things from the mortal cheerleaders. Things like discipline, coordination, timing, and the truth in that old adage "no pain, no gain."

Surely now our parents would understand why competition would be good for us, despite a few bumps and bruises. Mortal competition, where it doesn't pay to be sloppy because it hurts. Where you have to act as a team because bad things happen when you don't.

My hopes didn't seem so far-fetched when the crowd went wild. Even the angrier parents had grudgingly begun to clap and stomp when we got the crowd on its feet to cheer the team to another point.

Our Dragon Ball team won, but our cheerleading team won bigger. We could read it on the awed faces of our parents. I was sure we had made everyone understand how important it was to let us cheer.

But I should have known that such a massive insurrection wasn't going to pass unremarked—or unpunished—by Agatha, no matter what she promised the parents.

She vanished from the game the instant the game torch, lit by dragonfire, flickered out. She hadn't given us a ruling. Mom came up to me and hugged me. "Great job, honey. I think you've proven your point." I heard other parents saying similar things to their children. I let myself hope as we all gathered in the lunchroom at Agatha's again.

Unfortunately, Agatha didn't quite see it the same way we did. Sure, she lifted her moratorium on all things mortal. Her gracious decision was the first thing she announced when she appeared. "I am happy to announce that there is no longer a complete ban on competition with mortals."

Umm, yeah. While everyone else was cheering, I was in an eye lock with Agatha. I had understood the careful wording of "complete ban." When things had quieted down, I asked, "What about the cheerleading squad? Are we allowed to compete?"

"The cheerleaders will be allowed to cheer at mortal games, of course." Agatha went into full-on headmistress mode, and my expectations crumbled to dust as she spoke. "However, I'm sure your parents will agree with me that mortal competition is a risk that you do not have to take. It should be enough for you to cheer at games. Don't you parents agree?"

Of course, they did.

"But the whole point–" Tara tried to argue.

Agatha silenced her. "The whole point was to prove that you could cheer even more effectively. Which you proved. From what I saw, I don't think you need the small improvements a competition might give you." She killed our hopes with the worst kind of compliment. "You were wonderful. The teams you support are all lucky to have you rooting for them."

Right. Tell me she didn't know that wasn't what we'd been going for. Just in case she had any other kind of treachery on her mind, I spoke up again. "No detentions, though, right? We proved ourselves and our methods?"

She narrowed her eyes at me, making me glad I'd spoken up while the parents were still here to witness what she said. "Of course. No detentions will be issued for your passionate protest." She smiled. "However, I would like to let you students, and your parents, know that there is a new rule at Agatha's. In the future, any student caught participating in a—what was it you called it? a sit-in?—any similar action will result in that student being immediately expelled."

"Loophole closed but good," her expression said. As angry as I was, I knew we'd still been lucky. Our headmistress did not like to be outmaneuvered. I'm sure she would have managed to find a way to give us detentions, too, if I hadn't spoken up.

I hoped Agatha thought her end-run around fairness had worked and we were resigned to our fate. Not that we were, of course. We met at the pizza joint down the road to discuss what to do. Naturally, Tara and I were appointed to go talk to Agatha. As if that were even possible. But it was our duty, so we did it.

On Monday morning, Tara and I went to Agatha's office to plead our case. We went in uniform. We went prepared to beg, plead, bribe, cajole, and even threaten.

Agatha greeted us with her usually frosty manner. And then she shook her head. "Maybe we should never have allowed a cheerleading team at Agatha's. It was done against my better judgment in the first place."

That sounded like blasphemy to me. But, wisely, I didn't say so. We'd determined that Tara would do all the talking, since Agatha hated me. The only reason I was there at all was that both Tara and I felt that Agatha would notice my absence and that cowardice would count against us.

"Cheering teaches everything a good witch needs to know: independence, strength, perseverance, and teamwork." Tara was convincing–to me, at least.

It didn't matter what we said. Agatha had her mind made up. "You've already disrupted your schoolwork twice for competitions, and you haven't won either of them. May I suggest that your time would be better spent in analyzing how you can do what you suggested, and start a witch competition for cheerleaders. Then you can come back to me and I'll consider your proposal on its merits."

Right. The Witches would definitely win against the four other schools we could recruit from. They didn't even know the rules. But that wouldn't be the same thing.

"Out of my office, girls. We all have more important work to do than spend another moment on this silliness."

She waved us out. And that was that.

Or was it? I saw a gleam in Tara's eye just before Agatha banished us from her office. And I remembered why it was sometimes good to have a weeyotch in your corner.

Chapter 14

Samuel was not happy when he showed up to tutor me and found Angelo waiting by my side. He didn't even bother to smile when he witch-whispered, "No way."

"Not in front of the new kid," I witch-whispered back, and then added, so that Angelo could hear me too, "Let's get what we need from the potions cupboard before we start, Samuel."

I looked at Angelo and said, "You can start by opening your family spell book and finding a spell that will turn a rabbit into a goat."

"Okay." Angelo was very quiet and cooperative. I had a feeling he was screaming on the inside, but he'd been so badly bound by spells to keep his uncontrolled powers safely damped that he couldn't even manage to look miserable. He opened his family spell book, which was smaller and less dusty than ours (Mom had been given custody of his by the witches' council because of the no-contact-with-his-mother order).

We had barely popped into the potions cupboard when Samuel said, again, "No way."

I understood the natural aversion. After all, Samuel "liked" me, and I "liked" Angelo—or I had. And maybe I would again. But Angelo wasn't able to "like"—or be liked by—anyone right now. He was so beaten down that even dogs didn't like him much. He couldn't get much more harmless unless the witches' council decided to neuter him. Shudder. "Come on, you helped me."

He laughed, like I was comparing apples and oranges. "That's different. Your mom's a witch."

"So are Angelo's parents."

"The council's still out on that one." Apparently, he'd been listening to the school gossip machine, which was capable of mangling facts in a half-second flat. By the end of his first day, the top rumors were that Angelo had been found on another planet; that he was a plant by the mortals who suspected witches weren't just mythical; or—my personal favorite—that his mother had hidden him with mortals so she could go out and play with the other witches 24/7 and not be tied down to raising a kid. Ummm, I don't know who made these up, but boy are there some twisted minds in witchworld.

"Agatha's done the DNA." This was getting old. I mean, I understand the whole shock-and-denial thing—I'd had a little of it myself. But the facts were in. And Angelo was at Agatha's whether Samuel liked it or not. "He's a witch who was accidentally switched at birth and raised by mortals. Cut him a break already."

Stubborn could be part of Samuel's DNA too. "Maybe the testing was wrong."

"Wrong?" This was coming from the scientist? The genius who could make anything, including a Troll doll that talked like a butler and kept me on track for making all of my goals? Hah! "I didn't think you science types liked to clutch at straws."

He gave up his hold on the hollow hope that Angelo was not really a witch and was left only with the truth. "I don't like the way he looks at you."

Finally, something I could handle. Science was not my strong point—I could get an A on tests, of course, but I didn't retain much because it was so boring. "Samuel, do you want me to have my mom explain it to you? She was there at the hearing, just like I was."

He shook his head. Stubborn.

I sighed. "He couldn't help it. He manifested the Attractivity Talent without even knowing he was a witch. He's lucky we moved next door to him in time."

"I wouldn't call it lucky," he muttered.

"Who knows what might have happened?" I think I might have been flattered at Samuel's jealousy, except that To-Do was pinching me to make sure I had my study session, and I couldn't do that until Samuel agreed to let Angelo join us. He desperately needed to learn massive amounts of magic.

"Yeah. Just think. If you hadn't moved in here, you might never have met and set him up with Tara the Terrible."

I almost broke it to him that Tara was no longer interested in Angelo now that he was a witch with a zero on the personality scale.

"Setting Angelo and Tara up was a strategic move, and it worked, too. Didn't we get a spot at Nationals with our regional competition routine?"

Samuel nodded. "You guys are really good. Everyone could see it. Agatha really robbed you guys, not letting you go to the competition. You totally won the parents over."

"Tell me about it." I frowned. "Or better yet, tell me how you can help me find a spell to put Agatha in a good mood."

He laughed, lightening up at last. "That's not going to happen, so forget it. I think the last time she was in a good mood was at least five centuries ago."

Too true. "So could you try to be a little sympathetic here? You're trampling on big dreams of mine, you know."

"You've improved a lot. Although I think your magic

routines are so spectacular, I don't know why you can't give up this need to beat the mortal teams."

Oh no, not another voice of "reason." Good thing he was the one who'd instigated the sit-in. Otherwise I'd have to cross him off my friend list.

"Hey!" I let him know I wasn't going to tolerate that line of thought. "It's personal now. Me and Maddie. Tara and Chezzie. It's going down, on mortal terms, because that's the only fair way."

"It's not going down at all, Pru." He flipped his glasses at me before he said, ruefully, "Which I guess you could say are Agatha's terms."

I gave him the raised eyebrow of doubt. "We'll see."

"Are you going to try to change her mind again?" He shook his head like I was wasting my time.

Which I would have been, if I'd intended to try to change Agatha's mind. But that wasn't my plan. In fact, Tara and I had come up with a much better alternative. And I wasn't sharing with Samuel. "Agatha hates me. But we're going to that competition somehow, no matter what I have to do to get us there."

"And after?"

I grinned. "And after, Tara and I start lobbying for a competition for cheering witches. We'll have a good head start on the other teams. I bet we clean up in the win column."

"I bet you do too." He flipped his glasses at me. "You're

really amazing, Pru. Who knows what would happen if you turned your abilities on something that mattered?"

I resisted the urge to turn his hair green. I needed him. Angelo needed him. "You mean, something like science?"

"Exactly."

"That's your thing, Samuel, and I'm glad it is. You've gotten me out of more scrapes since I came to Agatha's than I ever thought I could get into."

He grinned. "You *are* good at getting into scrapes. I think it's because you want so much to be perfect."

I could feel him softening toward me, but he wasn't quite ready for me to ask about Angelo again. "What else should I aim for? Almost? Good enough?"

"Sometimes." He looked sad.

"Do you?" I regretted the question the minute it was out of my mouth. He ran errands for his own mother every week, and she didn't even know who he was. Of *course* he settled for good enough sometimes.

I'm sure he thought about her too, but he didn't mention it aloud. "Sometimes my stuff doesn't work perfectly. Look at the bracelet that tingled when someone was lying to you—it just made you miserable at your sweet sixteen sleepover."

"Well, of course there are problems. I didn't say you got to perfection, just that you aimed for it." I sighed. I hated explaining the obvious. "Just like Angelo. So be a friend and help him out like you helped me out when I was trying to figure out this whole witch school thing."

"I don't know." His resistance was wearing down, though, so I knew I was close to getting him where I wanted him.

"Angelo doesn't even have a mom and dad he can tell anything to. This whole switched-at-birth thing is a shock to the system. It sounds like something out of a soap opera and it's his real life." I appealed to Samuel's generous side. "We're all he has right now."

"You mean Tara's all he has right now."

"Not so much." I had to confess the true situation now, or he would assume that Tara would be someone for Angelo to lean on. "Now that he's not forbidden mortal flesh, she's gone a little cold on him."

"She has?" He didn't look happy, just as I'd predicted, but I could tell he was feeling for the situation Angelo was in. Samuel wasn't hard-hearted. He just wasn't sure he wanted to encourage Angelo-and-Pru-time. I totally understood. "So are you and he . . . going to go out?"

"You need to pay less attention to the ridiculous gossip. I can't believe you haven't heard the real deal. Agatha and the witches' council put a Talent damper on him until he gets up to speed. He isn't interested in me, and I'm not interested in him because . . . well, because we can't be right now."

He gave a low whistle. "I hadn't heard that," he said.

"Sucks to be him, now that the girls aren't all about catching his eye. Maybe we should convince him to pack up and head back to mortal world."

Awkward-moment alert. I sighed, prepared for it, and prepared to combat it. Maybe that was my Talent? Pru the Prepared? Gah. I hope not. First, it would be boring. Second, how would I demonstrate it at the Graduation Talent Pageant next year?

"I don't know. It must be a pain to have girls all over you all the time, even when you don't act like a player."

"I wouldn't know."

"Think about it"—I played innocent, with eye bats and all—"I mean, he gets a break from all that while he learns to handle his magic. No girls allowed."

"Some of us come by that naturally," Samuel sneered. He still wasn't getting the picture. He was too busy not feeling sorry for Angelo having to live the life Samuel had been living his whole high school career.

I decided to step it up a notch. "I guess it must be a relief, huh. Not to have girls always after you? More study time that way."

"Study time's good." He watched me, knowing I was going somewhere, but not sure where.

"Then maybe he'll be able to master his Talent and magic more quickly so that Agatha and the council lift the spells." I frowned, as if this wasn't a totally pleasant idea. "Of course, if he does, all the girls will want him again, including Tara. Then it might be just you and me studying together, like old times."

"I guess." He flipped his glasses once, then stopped. He smiled. Hah! He'd taken my point. At last. For a smart guy, Samuel can be slow at the old psychology math. One guy who attracts tons of girls, including his former girlfriend, just may equal one girl—me—left over for the geek who tutors the guy with the Attractivity Talent.

So maybe I was treading into dangerous territory again, making Samuel think he had a shot with me. If it happened, I'd handle it. After all, I almost had all my old Pru magic back. A little higher on the success chart, and I had a lock on being captain of the team next year. Perfect grades, or headmistress's favorite? Not so much. But one thing I'd learned in this whole turn-my-life-upside-down adventure was that a girl shouldn't be greedy. It's soooo last millennium.

Tara popped in to see me right after my study session with Angelo and Samuel. We'd agreed to meet outside of school, to avoid the risk of being overheard. Even the library wasn't safe, given that my mom was the librarian and she knew I'd never be caught there for something as simple as a book. Tara showing up here? That shouldn't set off any mom-alarms. She'd been doing it while we got ready for the Regionals, and even after. Nothing to see here, parents, move along now.

Which didn't keep me from looking around to make sure Mom hadn't popped in while I wasn't looking.

I stuck To-Do back in my pocket, having already agreed with him that I would recommence work on the newest routine I had thought up for Nationals. "Perfect timing! I just finished studying with Samuel and Angelo and I was just about to start sketching out this new routine. Want to see?" I waved my hand, and the routine glowed in the air in front of me.

"I like that." She watched for a second, but then quietly clued me in on the latest. "I've talked to everyone. They're in. The secret practices are a go."

I closed my eyes. "Perfect!" . . . and perfectly scary. I opened my eyes, suddenly worried. "Did you tell Charity, too?"

Tara shrugged. "Yep. I decided that she'd hear about the practices, anyway, and I don't want her to guess the bigger plan—which she would, for sure, if I kept this a secret from her."

"True." Sometimes the best way to keep gossip down is to pretend to tell the whole truth and that there's nothing left to hide. "So, you don't think anyone else knows we're planning more than secret practices?"

To-Do, at the mention of more time that needed to be scheduled, pinched me. I pulled his hair, which was a new feature Samuel had added—it gave me an hour until I had to update, and saved me from being pinched until I bruised when I didn't have time to update the schedule. The only downside was that To-Do inevitably said, "Goodness gracious!" in a proper British accent.

"Not a clue." She smiled at me with that look bungee jumpers get before the first plunge. "It's a big deal, Pru. Going up against Agatha. I hope you're up for it."

"Up for it? I can't wait." Secret practices were only the first step of our evil plan to thwart Agatha's evil plan. We were going to go to Nationals without school sanction. If Agatha had been worried I was going to corrupt the magic instincts of her students before . . . ? Well, let's just say her discovery of this broken rule would guarantee that she'd be justified—in her own mind, at least—in expelling me. But if I couldn't compete, I knew I didn't care.

Tara said, "That Maddie girl is so going to wish she'd never messed with you."

"She shouldn't have messed with a witch if she didn't want me to call her on being a backstabbing beeyotch. I'm going to enjoy taking her down," I agreed.

Unfortunately, I hadn't done a visual sweep for parents until one second too late. Dad was standing at the doorway, a tray of hot chocolate and cookies in his hands.

"Hi, Dad. Thanks!" I said, hoping he hadn't overheard.

Unfortunately, Dad *had* overheard. He didn't say anything while Tara was there, but afterward, he let me have it.

Being Dad, he had to have the conversation while Mom was in the room. While he started in, she just shook her head at me. "Pru, I'm disappointed in you. Do you think being a witch makes you better than Maddie?"

"Of course not. I was only kidding. She just dropped me like a rock when I moved."

"So your feelings are hurt and you want to get back at her. That's understandable. Have you ever thought about things from her perspective?"

Well . . . not until I spied on her from her closet, but that wasn't something I could admit to Dad if I didn't want to be grounded until I was two hundred years old.

"Pru. You have to give us mortals a break when it comes to understanding."

"Dad, *you* don't understand–"

"Maybe I do. You and Maddie have been friends forever. Don't burn your bridges because you moved away and things changed. Things always change. Look at me. Haven't I adjusted to living among witches?"

Well, come to think of it . . . "How did *you* flip from the 'not my thing' to the 'I'm cool with it' side? You're not even able to do magic."

"No. And for a long time, I thought magic wasn't necessary for anyone, witch or mortal. But I've seen the way you and Tobias have grown since we've moved. This change was the right change for you, no matter how hard it was."

That was almost like Dad saying he was wrong. Not an everyday occurrence in my house. "Sometimes I wonder."

"That's the human condition, whether we're witch or mortal. We're always wondering." He smiled. "But I can tell you, I'm sure that it has been good for you to live and go to school among witches. Get in touch with your witch side, so to speak."

"I wondered what mellowed you out."

"You did, honey." He looked serious for a moment. "But now I'm worrying that you're losing touch with your mortal side. I think it's time I do something about that."

I had the horrible feeling he was resurrecting his threat of taking me back to Beverly Hills. "I can't go back, Dad. I just can't."

"Not permanently. But I think a visit is just the thing." He hugged me. "People are like onions, Pru."

"They stink?" I'm not a big fan of onions—or my dad's lame metaphors, either.

"They have many layers."

"Deep, Dad. Did you use that one on an ad campaign?" Really, I have no idea why he's so creative at work and such a cliché-spouter at home.

He didn't get mad. "I've just learned that over the years. Think about where'd you'd be if I hadn't taken the time to appreciate your mother for all of her layers."

Pretty much nowhere. Which, I couldn't help thinking, might even beat being here right now.

"Let's ask your mom what she thinks," Dad said, looking

at Mom. "That way, you can balance your inner witch and your inner mortal with advice from your outer witch and your outer mortal."

That Dad. Sometimes I wonder how he ever made so much money in advertising. I guess cornball is where the money is.

Chapter 15

Mom sighed and put her book down. "You have been best friends with Maddie for so long, Pru."

I should have known Mom would totally back Dad up without letting him know that she was perfectly aware that Maddie and I were ex-BFF. She'd known the way the wind was blowing for quite a while. Mom was content to let me chill out anyone—as long as I didn't throw a zit spell on them. When she heard about *that*, she made me take it off.

Dad, however, believed in treating good friends like gold. He had no time for girl drama and never had.

You see, Dad had two older sisters, my aunts Sylvia and Donna, and he'd had all the girl drama he could stand by the time he was five.

Not that I was as bad as my aunts. No way. Mom even called them the Agony Aunts before they visited on Thanksgiving and Christmas. And Dad let her get away with it.

"I want you to call Maddie and make up," Dad said.

I looked to Mom to stop the insanity, but she nodded as if it was a fine idea.

"I am absolutely not going to make up with that back-stabbing crush-poacher!" I crossed my arms.

Dad started lecturing me, but I tuned him out. (Literally. I said a spell to turn his words into music.)

Dad stopped lecturing me about twenty minutes after he started. I thought I'd survived relatively unscathed, until I undid the spell that tuned him out and heard, "We're going to Beverly Hills for a visit. You haven't heard a thing I've said."

Mom, Dorklock (who'd wandered in to watch the carnage), and I did the whole freeze-frame thing.

Dad noticed and waved his hands. "Pru and I. Not all of us."

Dorklock unfroze and said, "Good. Hannah and I are scheduled for a tournament of champions, and I can't let her down."

Mom and I stayed frozen. I waited for her to shoot Dad down. Instead, she said, "Do you really think that's wise? We always said we wouldn't interfere in the children's squabbles."

Dad raised his eyebrow and looked at me. "Pru is not a child, she's about to be a young woman, and she needs to learn to be the best young woman she can be. Even if she is a witch."

Mom sighed. "True. We don't want to raise someone who would take delight in hurting others."

"Mom!" I thought maybe she'd forgotten the most important thing. "Maddie's a mortal, I can't apologize for the zit spell. Or the"—oops, she didn't know about the argument spell; fortunately, I recovered in a flash—"fact that I don't like how she snuck around behind my back and ended up with the boy she knew I had a crush on."

Dad really had made up his mind, though he didn't object to a little more lecture. "In this world, honey, there are two kinds of people: the kind who choose to hurt others, and the kind who don't."

Blah blah blah. And turn the other cheek. Blah blah blah. "I'm not a people. I'm a witch."

Dad shrugged. "Just because witches do magic doesn't mean they have to hurt others with that magic."

"It was no big deal. I didn't really hurt Maddie." I couldn't make myself sound too convincing. Maddie was going through a rough time with that boyfriend of her mom's ragging on her all the time. She probably could have used another friend—or, at least, not had to fight with her boyfriend all the time.

"Really? Then it won't hurt us to check it out." Dad so meant it. I thought, for the first time since I was two, about zapping him with a nice time-freeze until I was all grown up.

I knew he was serious, but I didn't know how serious until he asked, without a single twitch of his eye, "Pru, your mother was going to pop me to a meeting tomorrow in L.A. Why don't you just pop us there together, and we can work in a visit to see Maddie as well."

Okay, things were really getting weird. I knew Mom had been popping him instead of him flying—he said it gave him more time with the family—but this was my dad, asking *me* to do magic that included him. My dad, who still didn't trust me to drive him anywhere. Welcome to my life on an alien planet.

"Should I show up in their living room?" I didn't want to encourage him, but outright stonewalling never went well with Dad.

"That wouldn't be a good idea, now would it?"

Mom had decided to be helpful. "What about that nice hotel we put your parents in when they visited us in Beverly Hills?" Yay, Mom, way to problem-solve . . . soooo not.

"What if the room we go into is already occupied?"

Mom looked at me, then sighed. She swirled her finger in the air and made a tele-vortex. "Beverly Hills Arms, please."

"One moment." The nasal whine was barely finished before the ringing of the line began and ended.

Another voice, more welcoming, if a bit haughty, echoed in our living room. "Welcome to the Beverly Hills Arms. How may I be of service?"

Mom watched Dad's face as she answered. "I'd like to make a reservation, please." Even I noticed he didn't wince once.

"Certainly." There was the sound of tapping on a keyboard. "For when?"

Mom didn't hesitate. "Today."

The haughty voice frosted up, as if he thought this might be a joke. "Today?"

Mom lowered her voice, as if to prove she was truly sincere in wanting a reservation. "Yes, in an hour."

"Let me see if we have anything available on such short notice." More clacking on keys. This time I hoped he would say no. Not that I believed they were full. Just that I hoped they would decide, completely on a whim, that we were undesirables in their neighborhood. "Very well." Too bad.

"Excellent." Mom smiled at me. "I'd like to reserve Room 525, if that's possible."

"Let me see." There was some clicking. "That room is free. I have reserved it for you."

"Wonderful." Mom gave them the particulars, which

included Dad's AmEx number. She asked for a fruit bowl to be delivered, then said cheerfully, "My husband and daughter will see you in an hour then."

Dad gave her a kiss. "You're better than a secretary. Thanks for thinking of the fruit bowl." He looked at me. "Go pack, Pru."

"Why? We have to wait an hour."

Mom looked at me. "No, you have to pack so that you're there in an hour. And that means you need to hurry. Even being able to pop from one location to another doesn't mean you don't need prep time."

"Good old prep-time. Can't live without it." Dad swallowed once, hard, but he didn't wince. And then he smiled. "I'll bring my good suit so I can catch up with Harry while Pru mends fences with Maddie."

Mends fences. Hah. How about break them down and build a great big brick wall so tall, I couldn't scale it, even though I can fly.

We followed Mom's scenario, popping into the room she'd reserved for us so that we could be certain that there was no one in it. Then Dad went downstairs to formally check us in. Meanwhile, I was supposed to be using my cell phone to call Maddie. I'd gotten it back from Samuel with all the numbers intact. Not that I needed it. I'd had Maddie's number memorized for so long, I couldn't forget it—no matter how hard I tried.

She answered, which I hadn't expected, since she had to know it was me. There's not a lot of anonymity in the cell phone calling game. "Hi, Pru." She didn't sound all that friendly, but she wasn't hating on me either. Of course, she had no idea I was the one responsible for her recent inability to get along with the bf.

"Hi, Maddie. I'm in town with my dad for a whirlwind business trip of his." My cover story—I had been so used to thinking up cover stories growing up among mortals, I'd become a whiz at it. Living in Salem, mostly among witches, I'd gotten rusty fast. I guess there are things to appreciate about Agatha's. No cover stories necessary.

She was silent for a second, as if she was trying to decide how to handle the call. I suppose she was trying to think what to say to me. "Your mom let you skip school?" I guess she'd decided an apology wasn't going to cut it.

"As if." I said it without thinking, because I'd already had to switch around my scheduled study sessions. The trip wouldn't cut into school or practice time, which would have at least made it bearable. No, it would only make me have to study harder when I got back home.

Fortunately, Maddie filled in the blank with a mortal explanation. "In-service day, then?"

"You got it in one." I knew my tone was a bit cold, but really, she deserved it.

I guess she didn't agree, because her tone was just as cold as mine. "How nice you decided to call me."

Okay. Some snark going on there. But I can handle snark—I wouldn't be a good cheerleader if I couldn't. "I thought you might like to get a Frappuccino at the coffee shop. My dad's treat."

"I don't think so."

That was unexpected. Maddie never turned a Frappuccino down—that I knew of. Of course, people change a lot in a couple of months sometimes. I didn't know what to say.

She did, though. "Maybe next time you're in town?" Wow, she had the frost-beeyotch tone down almost as well as Agatha. And she wasn't even a witch.

There was only one thing to say to that. "Kewl." I grabbed an orange out of the fruit basket and ordered a movie.

At first I thought my cell phone was vibrating, but when I realized it wasn't, I remembered that Samuel had said tracking devices would vibrate when you got close to the person you were tracking. I was near Maddie, so I looked for the lip gloss, intending to throw it away. With my squad banned from attending Nationals, I had way more to worry about than what Maddie and Chezzie were up to. But then I felt the vibrating cardboard under my fingers and pulled out the card Daniel had given me.

When Tara and I had met with Agatha, I'd put a tracking

spell on the card Daniel had sent me. I'd hoped, if things went badly, I might find him and get him to convince Agatha. But I hadn't dared hope it would actually work.

I forgot everything Samuel had told me about trackers for an entire minute. During that time I just stared at the buzzing tracker, willing it to stop. Or not. It didn't stop buzzing.

Briefly I dreamed of what it might mean if I found Daniel. Me, tracker queen of the witches. Agatha my new BFF. Daniel . . . well, anywhere from sitting behind me in math to stuck in the quicksand of detention until he was a hundred.

Then I remembered that Agatha and all the witches' council couldn't track Daniel. The thing was probably malfunctioning. Still, as I watched it continue to buzz, I wondered . . .

I tapped the tracker and said:

"Take me there now.
Where, when, how,
No matter—
Take me there now."

I blinked and found myself on an L.A. street corner. I didn't see Daniel anywhere, but that wasn't surprising. There was a small crowd listening to a musician play, so I started scanning faces.

I didn't recognize Daniel's sly smile or even his fascinating eyes. The man closest to me was too old, the one across from me too fat. I looked at the women. Not really Daniel's style, but he was in hiding, so it would be foolish for me to rule that out and miss finding him.

I really did need an ace in the hole when it came to dealing with Agatha. Finding Daniel for her would probably make her agree to let us compete at Nationals. I don't think it would ratchet her up to grateful, but how could she not at least move to reasonable?

There were only a few men in the crowd, and the rest were women. Or looked like women. You could never tell in L.A., so I scanned closely, trying not to be too obvious.

They all seemed like women, not like Daniel in disguise. For a minute I was truly stumped, and then I focused idly on what had brought them all to a halt on this particular corner: There was a musician on the street, playing a saxophone in a smooth and sexy way.

I had dismissed him at first, because he was short and Daniel was tall. But then I noticed he was straddling a low wall. His face was painted in red and yellow diamonds, and his eyes were closed. There was something about the music, though, that kept me there, listening and looking and waiting for the musician's eyes to open, so I could be sure he wasn't Daniel.

As the music came to a halt, and the crowd drifted away, his eyes opened. It *was* Daniel. Sleepy, sexy, and definitely Daniel.

"Lovely music," I said, when he just sat there smiling at me.

"Thank you." He ran his fingers lightly along the saxophone. "My newest passion. Have you run away too?"

"No." I wanted to say something smoky and sexy back, to keep the moment going. Instead, I said, "I'm here with my dad to see my old best friend, the mortal who stabbed me in the back. I have to make nice with her because we Stewarts are supposed to treat our friends like gold."

I was appalled to hear myself babbling, but not all that surprised.

"And you just happened on me here? It must be fate."

I decided not to confess that I'd tracked him. Instinctively, I knew it would ruin the moment. Big-time. "Must be. Want a cup of coffee?"

He stood up and stowed the saxophone in its case, then slung it over his shoulder. "My treat, seeing as how you're my guest."

"That's okay, I—" I looked at the cup of change still at his feet, unsure how to indicate I knew he was poor.

He laughed when he saw me and picked up the cup to pour the change into his backpack. "Pru, I'm not mortal. I don't need money, except to pay for a random cup of coffee with a pretty girl when fate brings her to my door."

We found a seat at a table in the corner of the nearby coffee shop. Daniel, as always, made the space our own by putting a privacy bubble around us. We could speak freely, no witch-whispering necessary.

I hadn't known him very long before he'd run away from Agatha's, but seeing him here, like this, made me realize how much I'd missed him.

"Do you ever think of coming back? It would make Agatha happy." And my life easier, especially if I got credit for the prodigal's return.

"Sure. G isn't so bad."

I made a face that indicated I wasn't so sure.

He laughed. "To me, anyway. If only she'd lay off the family tradition stuff. She's killing me with the expectations of generations, you know what I mean?"

"Yeah. I hear you." I wasn't even happy to follow the witch tradition and move to Salem, so I wasn't just saying what I knew he wanted to hear. I felt his pain, and it was mine. Except, maybe, I had gotten lucky in the parent department. I tried to imagine what it would be like to have Agatha as a great-grandmother and failed. "I thought about . . . not running away exactly . . . but just refusing to move."

"You can still run, 666 Girl." Daniel smiled in a way that made me want to say okay. For a second.

"I'm not a runaway kind of girl." It was kind of a new realization. I guess there are some things you don't know about yourself until you find out in some random conversation. Weird.

"Too bad." He smiled. Still the sexy bad boy, I was reassured to see. Everything was changing on me so much, I liked it that one thing—Daniel and his bad-boy vibe—was still the same. And then he added, "I kind of hoped if you looked me up—"

"You knew I'd look for you?"

He shrugged. "Seventy-thirty odds in favor." He grinned.

Was he telling me he thought I was mega nosy? Or just a first-rate tracker? "But no one else has ever come close to finding you . . ."

"No one else has permission to find me."

Wow. All this time I'd thought I was so clever, but it was just that Daniel hadn't blocked my search. That was mind-blowing.

I looked at him. "No one else?"

He grinned. I couldn't help hoping he'd come back for senior year. And what did that say about me?

I tried, feebly, to encourage him to come home. It would make my life easier, but I knew in my heart it would make his worse. "Agatha misses you."

"G always misses me—until I return." His lips pressed together in that common expression reserved for relatives who love us so much, they drive us crazy. "I bet she blames you, doesn't she? Sorry about that."

"Mostly she blames me for everything—with good reason. I've done lots more bad things since you disappeared."

I told him everything—the cheering competition, reme-dial classes, my sweet sixteen, the works. The only thing I left out was Samuel's mom. He thought it was all hilari-ous. It was funny how easily I could still talk to him, even though he really had left me to Agatha's wrath when he'd run away from school and his family again.

We sat sipping coffee, facing the window instead of each other. We watched the beautiful people—and an occasional not-so-beautiful tourist—wander by the window. "Why did you stop sending me the anonymous notes, after that last one at Thanksgiving?"

"I figured you weren't ready to leave Agatha's behind."

"Of course not. I have to figure out how to be a witch. Do you know I still haven't manifested my Talent?"

"Horrors!" He threw up his hands in mock dismay. "She's Talentless."

"Stop it. Everyone has a Talent except me. Do you know there's even a witch who was switched at birth with a mor-tal baby and raised by mortal parents who manifested his Talent before me?"

He shook his head, crumpled his coffee cup, and tossed it into the trash can five feet away. "Oh, 666 Girl, you can do better than that."

No, I really couldn't. So I went back to the little things. Things he might like to know, even though they didn't matter. "My locker ghost has been very well behaved since you left."

"I imagine so, since you know his weakness was brownies."

"Nothing wrong with having a weakness for brownies." I felt a need to defend Hi. After all, he'd been stuck in the afterlife haunting a locker. How fun could that be?

"No, guess not." He prodded, just like I knew he would. Daniel the troublemaker at work. "Nothing wrong with running away, either."

"That's different. We do need to learn stuff, even if it's not always fun."

"Do we?" He sipped his coffee in silence for a few minutes. "School's just not for me. G doesn't get it. I'm a free spirit. I learn what I need to learn on the streets."

"Why in streets crowded with jaded mortals?"

"They're not as jaded as they seem, you know."

"No?" I had lived here for most of my life. "I think they're more jaded than you realize."

We talked for a while, long enough that we stopped looking out at the street and started looking at each other. I remembered why I'd gotten into the time bubble with him that first month in my new school. He'd been annoying, for sure, shooting erasers at my face in remedial summoning and spells. But he'd also looked at me. Tried to see through all the fashion and makeup disguises to the real me. Not many people will do that, or maybe I'd become cynical in Beverly Hills. But, really, who had done that in Salem except Daniel? Samuel, Maria, Denise. Tara was beginning to, but looking past the surface did *not* come naturally to her. Yet.

When my coffee had been cold for quite some time, he stood up. "Thanks for the coffee, and the blast from the past. Come back and see me sometime."

I wasn't thinking of Agatha when I said, "You come home." I was thinking of me. And of how much more I'd like to know about Daniel.

He just shook his head. "Not yet, 666 Girl, not yet."

He leaned in to kiss me. He did it slowly, so that I could duck if I wanted and his lips would land on my cheek.

But I didn't duck. The kiss was nice. It told me two things: one, there was no way I'd ever turn him in to Agatha without his consent; and, two, he was as totally wonderful a kisser as I'd remembered.

After a little while, he pulled back and said, "I see you've figured out how to deactivate your mother's protective spell."

"I'm a natural at this witch thing." I smiled at him.

"That, you are," he agreed. And then he left the table. I sat there and watched him from the window. He blended right in with all the other L.A. characters.

I sighed, and then detoured into the bathroom so I could pop myself back to my hotel room unnoticed by the mortals in the City of Angels.

Chapter 16

Maddie's brush-off was kewl with me, but Dad had other ideas. I watched as he called up Maddie's mother and got us invited for dinner. My only hope was that Maddie wouldn't be there.

No such luck, of course. Not only was Maddie there, so was Brent. And Maddie was mad. Not that she could let her mom, Armand, my dad, or Brent know.

Me, she let me know how she felt in the way only best-friends-turned-enemies could possibly understand. First, she was extra nice to my dad. I mean butter-the-toast-on-both-sides-and-don't-sweat-the-calories nice.

Get this: My dad said, "I hoped you and Pru could

mend fences. Good friendships are worth preserving, even over the distances."

Old Maddie would have smiled and nervously changed the subject. New Maddie? She just smiled and kissed him on the cheek. "You were always so wise, Mr. S."

Wise. Right. That's why he beamed at her like he thought she meant what she'd said. Sometimes my dad can be such a sucker, even though being in advertising, he should know better. For example, the way he seemed so delighted to see Armand, even though it was obvious the guy was a complete snake.

I gave Maddie the "gag me" sign behind my dad's back. Maddie just looked at me like I'd flashed my boobs to her bf. And then she said, "Pru, you're looking great! The porcelain skin tone works well on you. I guess it's not the East Coast thing to tan, huh?"

Beeyotch. "I just haven't had time, what with getting my team in shape for the national championships and all." I probably shouldn't have said anything, but she had her arm around Brent's waist, so I couldn't help myself.

"Nationals? Do you think that's wise? I mean, you know we're going to take it again this year, and coming in second place can be so hard on the ego."

I laughed as if her words didn't sting like an entire hive of bees. "Don't count your competitions until they're won," I said, echoing my old coach's saying—she didn't like us getting cocky too soon. She said that was the way to lose even worse than you thought you could.

I looked at Brent and Maddie, curled up together, and made an awkward segue. "We're going to do great, tanned or untanned. Anyway, my very cute and very distracting neighbor Angelo likes girls with milky skin."

Yeah, like I said, not the smoothest transition in the world. I just wanted to buzz Maddie back a bit. Technically, Angelo had said no such thing. Technically, Angelo was under so many heavy-duty spells and charms that he couldn't feel or say such things. So I was embellishing a little. But it's not a crime to add two and two, is it? I mean, Angelo likes me—or at least he did before Tara came on the scene and he found out he was switched at birth. I have milk-pale skin, ergo Angelo likes girls who don't live in a tanning salon.

Maddie didn't bother to pretend she didn't believe me. Ex-BFF can be like that sometimes. They know you way too well to fall for the stuff that other people would never believe you'd go to the effort to make up.

I lifted my purse, a tiny Coach bag I'd popped up because I knew how much Maddie had liked last year's version, and dug out my cell. "See? This is Angelo." I found my favorite and held up the phone.

Brent, who didn't know me at all, believed I was sincere and leaned in for a look. Maddie, who knew me way too well for comfort, frowned at him, then tugged on his arm. "Time for dinner."

I had never had dinner in Maddie's formal dining room. We'd once gotten into trouble because we'd made a princess castle under the massive oak table. We'd taped princess stars made out of silver paper all over the table legs, buffet, and the erstwhile clean glass front of the bar. And more than once we'd spied on a candlelit dinner party where the guests laughed and the glasses clinked and we pretended we were princesses trapped in the tower of a mean king and queen.

I guess maybe I should have realized Maddie wasn't making up her play fantasies out of fairy tales without weaving in some of her real life. But I'd been a kid then, and I'd assumed her parents were happy, like mine.

Instead, we'd always eaten in Maddie's room or at the big kitchen table that looked out over the hills. We'd told creepy stories about wolves and coyotes and mountain men who were looking to eat little girls. We'd had things like pizza and hot dogs, and—when her mom was on a vegetarian kick—carrot sticks with hummus and fresh fruit. Nothing like this fancy dinner of poached fish, glazed vegetables, and awkward silence.

Dinner got even more awkward after Armand had had his second glass of wine. It had been bad enough with Maddie and me at polite daggers up. But I stopped wishing that Maddie would sprout zits and break up with Brent right in front of us when Armand started talking like he was the king of this particular castle.

I looked at Dad, wondering how he felt about it. Armand was maybe thirty. Maybe. And he acted like he owned the house. Dad seemed fairly kewl with it, although I saw his eyebrows twitch once or twice when Armand said something along the lines of, "I don't allow laziness in my house." This, after he'd admitted he hadn't yet found the perfect career. I think he'd been trying to get my dad to offer him a job. You know, the kind of job that pays a lot and doesn't require you to work. As if.

I'm not sure about that, though, because I tuned out most of what he said right after he yelled at Maddie for chewing too loudly—which she totally wasn't. Dad's brows definitely furrowed at that one.

By the time dinner was over, I just wanted to bury the hatchet—in Armand—and run. Instead, I went into the little pink powder room off the kitchen and took the arguing spell off. Maddie wouldn't be compelled to fight with Brent anymore. It was the least I could do.

Except—no, there was one more thing. I quickly put the spell on Maddie's mom and Armand, with a little twist. I added a nice subtle touch to the spell that was just perfect for Armand. Maddie's mom would now smell the faintest whiff of skunk whenever he was near. It was the least I could do for the girl who used to be my best friend.

Under Dad's critical eye, I hugged Maddie and shook hands with Armand—his was sweaty and gross, yuck. "Thank you for dinner," I said to Maddie's mom. "I hope we can be friends again," I said as I hugged Maddie tight, for Dad's sake. I remembered old times, but I was pretty sure they were buried forever.

Maddie air-kissed my cheek—for Dad's benefit, of course. "I wouldn't have it any other way. See you at Nationals."

Nationals. Ummm. Yep. That was still a problem. Agatha had refused to talk to us, and our parents, while seeing the benefits of mortal competition, weren't willing to take Agatha on when her mind was so firmly made up. Most of them had gone to Agatha's at some point in their lives, so I guess I understood that—not that I approved of weenieness in general.

The gleam in Tara's eye had grown, though. She wasn't going to just follow the rules this time. "Agatha's moratorium is totally unfair, and we aren't going to stand for it." Or at least, that's what she wrote in the air in the locker room before practice—and then quickly wiped it away so no one but we cheerleaders would see it. Step two in our plan was underway.

We were already meeting for secret practices, so it was easy to get some private time to talk to the rest of the team. Even though Tara was over Angelo, she talked him into having the meeting at his house. His mother made good cover, being clueless about witches and all. The witches' council wasn't going to question a bunch of witches hanging out with another witch—after all, he had to quintuple time his education, didn't he?

All the girls felt sorry for Angelo and his situation, though none of us could understand why we had found him so hot in the days when we thought he was a mortal. Maybe out of pity, or kindness, everyone gave him freebie tips and showed him how to deal if his mom accidentally caught him doing magic.

I have to say, he was smart and caught on quick—maybe even quicker than I had. Maybe.

We gathered at his house after practice. Mrs. Kenton was a little in awe of the number of girls who wiped their dainty feet on her big welcome mat. I think she wasn't completely sure that sending Angelo to Agatha's was such a great idea anymore. Too bad, though. He was a witch and there was nothing she could do about it, even if she didn't know it.

Despite the secret location of the meeting, we maintained levels of security that usually only happened for those on the council. We passed notes around to one another, written in invisible ink on self-destructing paper. We'd have written in the air, like we did in school, but we didn't want to have to mind-wipe Mrs. Kenton. We felt safer just misdirecting her and blocking what she saw and heard.

We also used privacy spells. Many of them. Individual and group. I had scoured my family's spell book for two good ones myself. Paranoid? Maybe. But we were planning a fait accompli that required utter secrecy to pull off, and that was enough to make us not want to be overheard by anyone. Witch, human, or—especially—parent.

Our first hurdle was convincing Charity. Tara and I had decided that she had to be onboard, if we could get her. If not, we had a charm ready to make her forget everything she heard in practice until after the national competition.

Tara began with what was the most compelling argument for most of us. "Agatha's treating us like babies, and our parents are letting her get away with it."

I backed her up. "They really don't get how important competing is to us, you know." I used a little of the wisdom I'd gleaned from the mortal world. "Even mortal parents don't always get why cheerleading is so important to us. But we can't let them get in our way."

Tara tag-teamed me. "Right. If they don't get it, it's our job to show them."

The rest of the girls were starting to get over their fear of Agatha the frozen witch of the Northeast. They were thinking. Celestina even dared a question. "How can we show them if they won't even give us a chance to compete? I mean, we were fabulous at the magic game. My dad even said so—he said fabulous!"

"Our best chance is to come home with the trophy." Tara stood up and conjured an image of a trophy into her hands. She held it up. "What parent can argue with a trophy won fair and square?"

"That's going to get us in trouble with Agatha." Charity was looking at Tara, but I know her words were aimed at me—after all, I had been in trouble with Agatha from the moment I first met her.

"Exactly. Maybe it's time to challenge that old witch. She has our parents cowering, even though they know we should be competing. We can win, and she's holding us back," Tara declared.

"We are pretty good, now that we have Pru's new routines. I really liked the fountain." Elektra, bless her, had something positive to offer. Still—

"Pretty good?" It wasn't time for faint praise. I stood up next to Tara. "We're great. We aren't just going to impress our parents, we're going to impress every last judge on the judging panel—and our rival teams. So what if they're mortal? They'll still be jealous of our style, our sass, and our synchronicity. And the other cheerleaders are going to want to know how we do it."

"They'll watch us." Celestina looked worried. "What if they get better than us?"

Elektra waved her hand to dismiss the worry. "Don't be silly. First, we're light-years ahead of them, and we're great. Second, no one else has our secret weapon: Pru."

Sunita still wanted to do things the "right" way. Which meant with Agatha's permission. "What if we still can't convince Agatha?"

I made our objective clear to them all, at last. "Then it's time to show her we're not babies."

Charity looked a little worried. I got the charm ready, just in case. "What does that mean?"

Tara took over. "It means we go to Nationals, no matter what."

"Disobey our parents?" Jakeera didn't sound totally opposed to the idea.

Tara grinned. "Yep."

Charity frowned. "Risk Agatha expelling us?"

Tara frowned back. "Yep. Isn't it worth it?"

I held the charm in my left hand while Charity chewed her lip. "I don't know."

Tara stood up to indicate the time for discussion was over. "We all have to make the decision for ourselves. Are you in, or are you out?"

We all said, together, "I'm in." Even Charity. Eerie how our voices blended into one. I couldn't help but hope we were that on point when the time came to make it all happen.

Failure is not an option, but it's always a possibility.

We joined hands and I asked, "Agreed, then? We'll all meet at Nationals?"

"What do I tell my mom?" It was meek little Sunita who asked the question. But I don't think she was the only one wondering.

Fortunately, I had an answer, one that had proven effective for me in the past. "You tell her nothing."

"That should work."

Some of the girls looked happier than others, but no one said another word about getting around parents. That was not a new skill to witches in high school, apparently.

"What about Coach Gertie?"

"We can't get her involved," I said. "Her job is on the line. Agatha would never let her coach again. She might even fire her from teaching." Coach Gertie was also our assistant scrying teacher.

"Not that that would be a big loss. She's not the best at scrying," Charity said.

"Got that right." Elektra had almost failed the class, and was convinced it was because Coach Gertie had mistakenly told the entire class to clean their scrying crystals with Windex.

"She is a good coach, though," I pointed out.

"Okay. No Coach Gertie," Tara said. The rest of the girls nodded in agreement.

We were going to do it.

Chapter 17

There's something about sneaking that makes everything more exciting—even a cheerleading competition. I wouldn't have believed it, but it's true.

We showed up in the hall at the prearranged time, only to find Coach Gertie there. Busted.

For a minute, as my heart beat against my rib cage and my toes curled in shock, I wanted to pretend we were only there to watch, but Coach Gertie wasn't having any of that. "Nonsense, girls. I'm delighted to see you here. I just finished a meeting with Agatha. We have permission to compete. Is everyone here?"

The other girls got all excited at the news. I'm not sure why. Coach Gertie was a terrible liar, and I didn't believe for a second Agatha had given us permission.

I almost said something, but then Coach Gertie gave me a look that said, "Don't bust me." So I didn't.

What difference did it make, anyway? We had been about to break the rules. Now Coach Gertie was stepping between us and the big speeding bus of wrath that was Agatha. It probably wouldn't slow her punishment down much, but you never know. Plus, we were all together, Coach and team. What could be better than that?

The phrase "got your back" is great. I love it, especially on competition day. We, as a team, had one anothers' backs. We were set to win, and we were feeling good about our skills. There's something about going through a big fight together that bonds a team tight.

I looked at the stands, knowing that my parents wouldn't be there because they didn't know what we were doing. I'd only told one person. Samuel. Another Saturday's worth of time he'd missed with his mom. I looked at Maria and Denise beside him. What didn't I know yet about them?

That made me think of Angelo, who was struggling like me. And that's when I noticed he was there too! Sitting right next to Maria. I shot Samuel a big smile. He'd come through for me again. We were all trying to win the competition—the one that went on in our lives every day—in our own ways.

I watched them all sitting in the stands, waving at me. They were wearing our colors, smiling and waving wildly—

well, except Denise, who was not wearing any of our colors but black and who was definitely not smiling. Still, they had our backs, and it felt great.

I waved, but didn't go over. It was team-unity time. This was our challenge, and we needed to face it together.

Celestina was pale, but her grip on my arm was strong. "Pru, I'm going to do it. I know I can. Don't cut it out of the routine."

"Are you sure?"

"I'm sure."

I gestured to Tara, who leaned in. "Celestina says she wants to do it."

"Okay. Leave it in, then." She held up a big white number thirteen. "We're lucky number thirteen."

We grinned at one another, as wide as we could. Thirteen. A lucky number for a team of witches.

"Wonder what number they are?" Sunita asked. Tara had managed to turn the whole team to the common goal of beating my old team. It felt good to have us all on the same page.

"Who cares what number the losers have?" We laughed. It felt great to act like we were invincible.

It turned out they were last. There were twenty-five teams competing. We were thirteen, and then we'd have to wait through twelve more routines before we knew how we'd stacked up. If we were lucky, we'd then go head-to-head with my old team. I pitied the other teams that would end up in the final five. They didn't have a chance.

"I'm going to pop out for some pizza," Sunita said. She was a stress eater, big-time.

"No." I shook my head. "We have to watch the other teams. We have to practice, and we have to be mortal, just for today."

"Sounds like overkill to me." Charity. Of course.

"Trust me." I looked at them all. We'd come so far, but I was really just another member of the team, not head cheerleader, so they didn't have to listen. Everything could fall apart in a nanosecond if we started to break apart. "For today, we're a team, and we do everything as a team. Okay?"

It was a tense five seconds for me while everyone blinked and looked at Tara. But then they all shrugged—together, like a team—and said in unison, "Okay, Pru, whatever the cheer-whisperer wants."

"Great! Because what I want is"—I pumped my fist in the air—"to win!"

The first twelve teams were good, but only two were really good and none were great. I didn't see anything at all like the new signature move I'd designed for the team, which made me hope it would be enough to take our routine from very good to great—if no one choked, of course. But I wasn't going to let that negative thought into my head on competition day.

When they called us, I witch-whispered to everyone, "We're the Witches, watch us bewitch the world!" We ran onto the competition floor with smiles that were not only wide, but genuine.

"Hit your mark," I whispered, and we did. "Signature witch," I reminded them, and we all twisted sideways and crouched low. "Back left," I said, and Sunita started coiling upward, hands in the air, with each girl following her in a one-second delay that made a sinuous ripple through our ranks, like a moving snake. The crowd showed their approval with a murmur.

"Let's wow them! Center out." From the center this time, we pulled away to leave our three best stunters to do triple blackflips while the rest of us continued to undulate in a motion slower than the normal cheer move, but timed to perfection to go with our music—which was a cheesy, but appropriate "We Belong," by Pat Benatar.

From my years on a championship team, I knew the judges didn't like disjointed routines, so I'd tweaked the signature move so we could do it five times during our routine: opening, first stunt, third stunt, last stunt, closing. The song only lasts so long, there's no time for errors. We hit every time, but the best—even better than I'd imagined, never mind than we'd done in practice—was when we did the signature move as we threw four flyers into the air and they did forward diving flips in the air. It was a kewl effect, and the crowd roared.

I went with my instincts and said, "Let's give that to them again." We did, and the crowd roared louder. We didn't even have to cut anything from the routine, we just did our final bow quickly rather than with a drawn-out flourish as we'd planned.

"We were perfect! We have to win!" Sunita said as we ran off the floor, past a stunned-looking team number fourteen.

Tara, more realistic, asked, "So do you think we have a shot? Really?"

"I think we do." I didn't want anyone losing the team spirit, though. "But while we watch the rest of the teams compete, we should think about what we can do better next time, in case we make it to the top five."

Charity frowned at me. "Like what? We were perfect."

I shrugged. I didn't want to come off like a shrew. I just wanted to lift the bar a little higher. "Like flyers higher in the air so they can do two front diving flips instead of one."

"That's impossible." Elektra was our strongest base, and gave most of our height when tossing flyers.

Tara was having none of that. "Nothing's impossible. We're here, aren't we? We competed, didn't we?"

We watched, and learned a few places where we could push the cheer envelope. But our attention sharpened when my old team came up to take the floor.

Chezzie had tried harder to tweak my routines for

Nationals, but I think she'd made a few mistakes. She crammed in extra coordinated backflips, which would give her points for difficulty but lose her for overall sychronicity—girls can coordinate backflips well, unless there are too many and the different recovery time for each girl throws off the timing. Which is what happened to them. Not that the crowd noticed, but I saw the judges making notes.

"They're still better than us," Sunita said.

"Bite your tongue!" Tara ordered, back to being head cheerleader bossy now that we'd pulled off our sneak compete without a sign of Agatha. She smiled at Coach Gertie, and I realized that even Tara had believed Coach Gertie's lame lie.

I wondered if I should clue her in, but just then they announced they'd be naming the top five. We were one of the five. I don't know why I wasn't more surprised, but it just felt right as we marched out to sit on the floor like the team we were.

That was enough for me, just being in the top five. We'd come so far in only a few months, I wanted to cry.

I glanced over and saw Tara and Chezzie eyeing each other. I smiled, happy to leave the posturing to the head cheerleaders. I looked for Maddie. She was looking right at me. I hesitated a second, but then I gave her a sign we had used when we didn't want anyone else to know what we were saying. I tugged on my ear. Luck. She tugged on her ear. Luck.

I looked away and noticed that Chezzie was watching us with a puzzled frown. I couldn't help being glad that Maddie hadn't yet shared that special signal with her.

We'd wished each other luck. And I think we'd both meant it. Because when we took the championship with a routine so perfect, it shone, I could hear Maddie shouting, through the roar of the crowd, "Way to go, Pru."

Unfortunately, we had no time to enjoy our win. We looked out to the crowd, held up our trophy, and saw Agatha. She wasn't dressed all in white, so for a moment I thought I was mistaken. But then Coach Gertie saw her. She turned pale and began to sputter.

Agatha stood up, time-freezing the gym full of mortals with a single lift of her hand. She thundered, "Are you happy with your act of insubordination?"

No one said a word, not even Coach Gertie.

Were we happy? Well, yeah, I was. But was I going to say so?

"What have you got to say for yourselves?"

I looked at Agatha, standing there in jeans and a yellow sweatshirt that I think she must have borrowed from one of the "fashion don't" columns in *People* magazine.

I knew I should keep my mouth shut. I knew that the competition high made it dangerous for me to say anything.

I knew it. But, hey, a girl's got to live dangerously some-times, and today seemed the day for it.

"I like the vacation from all white. But really, Agatha, yel-low's not your color. You're definitely a winter, not a spring."

Chapter 18

I wasn't terribly shocked to be suspended pending Agatha's ruling on our insubordination. I'd expected to be expelled immediately, but apparently Agatha wanted to prolong the torture. Until she decided to bring her gavel down directly on my head, I had a lot of free time, so I devoted it to helping Angelo get up to speed.

Angelo and Samuel and Maria and Denise and I were hanging out, trying to teach Angelo how to summon more than five objects at a time.

"Too bad you can't fulfill Agatha's biggest dream and make Daniel a star student. Then maybe she'd get off your case," Denise said.

"Maybe I can." I said it, but I knew I didn't mean it.

Daniel wasn't ready to come back. And I wasn't going to make him. Not everyone was cut out for the rat race that was Agatha's.

Fortunately, no one knew that I was seriously able to find Daniel—if he hadn't terminated his permissions for me to seek him out, I guess. Even Angelo laughed, and he'd only been at the school for a few weeks.

I was really getting tired of the lack of respect I was still getting. "Seriously. Samuel taught me this kewl tracking spell. What if I could use it to find Daniel?"

Denise pointed out the obvious. "The entire investigative branch of the witches' council can't find him, and you think you can?"

Well, yeah, I knew I could. Not that I was going to share that 411. "I know him better than they do."

Samuel shook his head and sighed as if I were disappointing him in a critical debate team match. "Pru, you only knew him for a few weeks before he disappeared again."

I hadn't mentioned the anonymous notes he'd been sending me, never mind the coffee we'd shared in L.A. Something told me to keep it quiet still. "I know. But he's not far from the angry child stars who can't hack high school. I think I might have an idea or two about his whereabouts that those fuddy-duddy types would never dream up."

"Confident, aren't you?"

"Hey, who got the cheering team an invitation to Nationals, huh?" Not to mention a win. But I was playing modest today.

"You definitely deserve the title of cheer-whisperer, Pru." Denise, as always, thought little of the sport of cheering, preferring messages negative, or at the least, subversive.

"Thanks. I'm going to take that as a compliment." And I intended to too, because I knew that was guaranteed to drive Denise up the wall.

Maria, of course, always thought of others. "What if Daniel doesn't want to be found? I wouldn't, if I had Agatha in my family tree."

"He has to come back and face the music sometime," Samuel said, with more satisfaction than was seemly.

"Really? Is that always a good thing?" I was thinking of his mom, and his visits. I hoped he never faced the music for those. I hoped no one ever caught him either.

Denise argued, so I didn't have to, "Agatha isn't going to get the monkeys out for him."

Samuel wasn't going to give up so easily. "She might."

"No way. The love of a mother for her son—or a grand-mother for her great-grandson—is just too strong." I looked at Samuel while I said it, so he knew I was talking to him.

He got it. "Yeah. There are some bonds that shouldn't be broken, no matter what. Never mind, I give up. Daniel and Agatha—I hope they figure it out someday."

"What are the monkeys?" Angelo hadn't seen much yet. He didn't even know about detention in witch school. I probably shouldn't have taken so much glee in telling him, but, hey, I had to serve detention once, and if I could keep him from the same fate, consider me Public Service Pru.

"Wow." Angelo shook his head. "Who'd have thought *The Wizard of Oz* would have got it right."

Samuel and Maria just smiled. Denise, as usual, didn't waste time being polite. "They didn't. The monkeys have only been monkeys since the movie went blockbuster."

"What were they before?" I asked.

"Oh, they were dragons, in my mother's time. And Puritans once, with rocks and hanging ropes."

"Yeah. They go in for scary. Like the dementors in *Harry Potter*. You know, what we fear most. Having the life sucked out of us, being picked up by flying monkeys and swooped up into the air."

"So even at Agatha's, things change," I reflected.

"I guess you could say that. But not a lot. I mean, your mom was librarian once long ago, and now she is again."

"Some things were not meant for déjà vu moments, if you know what I mean." She'd fined me for one overdue book already. You'd think there'd be an advantage in having your mother be a librarian, but there isn't. And since witches don't use money, a library fine is an hour of dusting off the old books of magic, myth, and the spell books of families that no longer practice magic.

Agatha made us sweat it out until our third class of the day on Monday, when she summoned the whole team into her office, whipping us out of class without a second's worth of warning.

"I have decided on the punishment for your going to the competition against my express orders."

"We won!" Tara was front and center on this protest, and I was happy to let her take the lead.

"And what would give you the impression that winning some mortal competition would make me overlook your flagrant disobedience?" Agatha asked frostily.

Tara shrugged. "Maybe that you'd be proud of us for doing so well?"

Agatha sighed and then shook her head. "You all have detention, except for Prudence Stewart, your ringleader."

"What?" everyone chimed in, with a mingled horror and relief. We'd really thought we'd get expelled at the very least.

Agatha ignored the question and stared at me. "You, Miss Stewart, will be tried by the council on the charge of corrupting the magic of underage witches." She couldn't help smiling, she was so pleased. "I trust, despite your woeful ignorance of our witch laws and customs, you realize that this is a grave charge and one you should take seriously?"

Elektra was outraged at the injustice. "We won the competition, you know. We were the best. She taught us how."

Agatha had lost the last of her small store of patience. "Did you use magic?"

"Of course not."

"Meaningless."

We looked at one another. Not meaningless. Not at all. But that was all we got to register before we were out of Agatha's office and I was home, still suspended, waiting for a trial by council.

Even Mom didn't have a lot of encouragement to offer. She and Dad were proud of me for standing up for what I believed in, but they weren't exactly thrilled about my deceiving them. It was chore duty to the max until the council hearing.

This time my trip to the witches' council *was* about me. All about me.

I had hoped never to see the witches' council again. But here I was, back again, about to be expelled for being a bad witch. I didn't know that was even possible until I found out it had happened to Samuel's mom. I would have been more scared, but since I'd visited her, I wasn't.

She lived okay, even if she didn't know her own son anymore. She was old, but that was just because she'd lived for almost two hundred years before she was expelled by the witches' council. She was a smart lady, she loved her gardens, even the fake winter garden. She loved her tea and chats. She was happy.

I would have said so when the council spotlight hit me and I was asked to defend myself, but that would have gotten Samuel in deep doo-doo. So instead I said, "Look, I know I'm supposed to be all knock-kneed and willy-whispering about the idea of living out my life in the mortal world. But, hey. I've already done it. I can do it again. It doesn't scare me."

They did not look like my argument had suddenly changed their thoughts from gloom and doom to sweetness and light. In fact, I think I would have gotten a better result if I'd mooned them all. I braced myself for the flying monkeys, or whatever thing they'd think would scare the mortal-raised me the most. Maybe cut-rate plastic surgeons with dull scalpels. Yikes. I shut down that thought quick.

The old lady in red looked at my mother and shook her head slowly. "We knew no good would come of allowing you to marry a mortal."

"Pru was a little behind when she arrived at Agatha's—" Mom stopped while Agatha snorted in disbelief several times. "But in less than six months she has caught up in her lessons, created what we all admit is an excellent cheerleading squad, and been a serious witch in every way possible."

Agatha leaned forward. "Except one: She has corrupted

our youth and introduced them to an element they are far too young to understand."

Mom wasn't having any of that. "The mortal world is not like it is on TV. You know that as well as I."

"Of course I know that," she thundered. "Mortals are even more dangerous than they seem on that infernal television—blast Edison and his incessant inventing. I told him it would come to no good, for mortals or witches, but did he heed me? Of course not."

"TV has its good points," I said. "We all get to see things from other people's point of view."

Kilt Guy harrumphed. "Who needs to do that?"

"It helps to know why some girl might not think a manicure is a must-have—I mean, if she's into playing football or climbing trees, I totally get that the nails just aren't going to stay nice and smooth and polished."

Old Lady in Red looked like she was going to make her face and eyes match her outfit. But she looked at my mother. "Do you not see the outrage in this? She takes our children among mortals to have their nails trimmed and polished, to have oils rubbed in to soften their hands."

"And pedicures for our feet, too, don't forget." I knew it wasn't wise, but this was a trial and I wanted to be accurate. If I got off for manicures, I didn't want to be hauled back here because of pedicures. "And a little waxing, a few massage sessions. No big deal."

"For mortals." Old Lady in Red looked at me sternly. "But we are not mortals." She sent her voice, only a whisper, to echo and bounce off the walls. "We are all witches."

Agatha said. "Are we all?"

The room began to buzz.

One of the judges who hadn't said much before, the one I thought of as Stud in Black, leaned forward. "I think we've established that fact, given—"

Agatha interrupted him with a grand accusation, accompanied by a pointing finger: "She hasn't manifested a Talent yet, and she is well into her sixteenth year."

More buzz. Louder. Old Lady in Red raised her hands and sent a cloud of silencing steam toward the gallery of onlookers. Their buzz died at once.

She looked at me. "Is this true?"

"It is." I said. "But Mom says—"

Mom interrupted. "I think Prudence may be mistaken. I believe she has manifested her Talent, but she hasn't realized it yet."

All of the council members looked skeptical, but Kilt Guy was the one to ask, "How is that possible that no one had noticed? The girl has a schoolful of teachers, and Agatha—"

Agatha broke in, her wrinkled jowls waggling happily. "I have seen no hint of a Talent. Unless you count mischief with mortals as a Talent."

"It is a rare Talent," my mother said, bowing deeply to first Agatha and then Old Lady in Red. "One that only the most powerful of witches possesses."

"Impossible." Every member of the witches' council stood and spoke the word at once. It bounced into the gallery and back again. I looked at Mom, wondering when she'd lost her mind. But then I remembered how she'd been the one to spot Angelo as a witch. Maybe I did have some rare Talent. But I didn't have a clue what it could be.

"Demonstrate this Talent," Old Lady in Red demanded, looking right at me.

I smiled, as if I knew what my mother was talking about—this was definitely the time to have her back, even if I did think the stress had fried her brain. "I'm happy to. Perhaps we could arrange a time next week–"

"Now!"

I don't think I'd felt as clueless since my sweet sixteen party, when I'd ordered pizza in a room full of witches by using the mortal telephone. No, this was about a hundred times worse.

I stood for a moment, mentally preparing myself just like I did for a game or a competition. I closed my eyes and took a deep breath.

I had no idea what I was going to do next, so I was grateful when Mom said, "Wait, Pru. Open your eyes and wait a moment."

I happily obeyed, glad for a nanosecond's reprieve from yet one more disgrace.

Mom whipped her arm up to the big, domed ceiling of the council chamber and suddenly there was a movie playing up there. Only it wasn't a movie, it was the Nationals—it was us. It was me up there on the ceiling, right before we'd gone out to the floor to perform our award-winning routine.

"Do you know what they call her?" my mother asked. "They call her the cheer-whisperer."

"I don't see how that's relevant—whispering is not a Talent."

"Of course it isn't a Talent. But it does give you a hint of Pru's Talent."

As my mom spoke, the movie Witches gathered in a circle to do our rally hold and chant. Mom waved her hand and stopped the action. "I'm going to enhance this, to make it clear to everyone in the gallery."

I was glad. I hoped it would give me a clue too.

Suddenly, on the movie, all of our auras appeared. I guess Mom had done an aura reveal spell. I didn't know you could do that on a movie of something that happened in the past. Which made me realize that not only did I not know what my Talent was, I didn't know a lot of other kewl and useful things.

Mom started the movie going again, and I noticed a

weird thing: My aura danced and darted around with all the other girls' auras, until all the auras were dancing and darting and braiding into one strong and united aura. The team aura, made up of all our auras, glowed brilliantly as we worked in perfect synchronicity, and—well, it made me so proud, I started to cry. Everyone else was buzzing, but I still didn't see the big deal. So what if I had an aura that knew how to form a braid? So did everyone else on the team.

"How can you be sure that this is Prudence's work? It could be Tara's, or Coach Gertie's." Agatha leaned forward, clearly unwilling to accept that I was Talented.

Mom replayed the scene in slow motion. This time, there was no doubt that my aura began the dance, controlled the dances of the other auras, and was responsible for braiding everyone else's aura together into one mega-aura.

Kilt Guy looked at me with new respect. "The Magic Talent of an aura braider hasn't been seen since—wasn't it your great-grandmother, Agatha?"

"Yes." She didn't sound happy to admit it, though. But she looked at me with something I'd never seen in her eyes before. Sing it with me now: R-E-S-P-E-C-T.

I not only had a Talent, I had the kewlest Talent ever. Only question was, would it save me?

Old Lady in Red didn't bother with silencing the gallery crowd. She just waved them away. Back to whatever they had been doing, I presume, but I spent the next few moments of silence wondering about it because to wonder about me was way too scary.

"I'm surprised you didn't note this at once, Agatha, given your experience with the Talent." She looked at me with a little shake of her head. "Not to mention Miss Stewart's rather unprecedented talent—small t—for convincing the other students to work together. There was the fund-raising calendar they did at Halloween. I saw that in your evidence against her, did I not?"

Agatha nodded. "That was minor, compared to arranging for her team to practice in secret and sneaking off to a forbidden competition with mortals." She sniffed. "However, it does indicate her lack of a proper witchly attitude."

Stud in Black laughed. "Or perhaps it was the first warning sign that her Talent needed to be recognized and properly trained."

Kilt Guy nodded. "Exactly. To have this child in your school, under your nose, and to miss this? Especially after the sit-in episode? Perhaps you have been headmistress too long."

Agatha, for the first time since I had known her, turned a pale shade of pink. "I beg your pardon! I have done all I could to contain this girl. I insist she be expelled."

Old Lady in Red turned to look at her. "Do you? Insist? How interesting."

She turned back to Mom and me, still looking grave.

"Obviously, we cannot allow Prudence to continue to tes-tify, given the powerful nature of her Talent and the fact that she has not been trained to handle it. We must con-tinue our discussion in closed session, I'm afraid."

Mom said, "I would like the chance to speak for my daughter, if she can't do it herself."

"No need. You have already spoken eloquently, with your demonstration." Old Lady in Red raised her hand to dismiss us. "We'll take your evidence under advisement and let you know our decision posthaste."

We were back in the kitchen before the words had fin-ished echoing around the council chamber.

Sassy leaped into my lap as I sat there, staring at Mom, speechless, clueless, and suddenly not so happy that I might be leaving this whole witch thing behind me.

Chapter 19

The council didn't call us back to let us know their decision. Instead, Sassy coughed up a hairball at my feet. It rose into the air and formed the wiry message:

> Prudence Stewart has been determined to pose no grave threat to the youth of Agatha's Day School for Witches. She has also been determined to have manifested the rare and unusual Magic Talent of Aura Braiding. We expect a great deal of her from now on. Please convey our expectations to her, with our warmest congratulations.
>
> Best regards,
>
> The witches' council, decision unanimous
>
> cc: Agatha, Headmistress, Agatha's Day School for Witches

I blasted a shriek so loud through the house that everyone came running. We whooped as a family at the hairball/message from the council.

Dad hugged me. "I knew you would do it, Pru."

Mom waved the hairball into a frame. "Just to preserve the evidence," she said, when we all looked at her like she was crazy.

So I was reprieved. Me. Innocent. I should probably have been relieved, but Sassy's hairball had interrupted a session of summoning that Angelo, Samuel, and I were into in a very intense way. Not to mention I had a whole new action item to add to To-Do: learning how to manage my Talent.

Hey. Guess what! I'm Talented. Me. At last. And, best of all—it's a good one. I'll be able to stand out at the Graduation Talent Pageant. What a load off my mind.

Life is easier when you know your Talent. Especially when it's a rare and kind of kewl Talent like mine.

Take school, for example. The same teachers who looked at me as if I might be too dumb to pass a class now think I'm a star witch. If I get something wrong, they give me the benefit of the doubt. It feels a little strange, since I've gotten used to having to prove myself every day—heck, every hour. But it also feels a little bit back to the way it was in Beverly Hills, where the teachers took it for granted I was smart and capable.

There's one difference, though. Now that I've seen the way my aura can reach out and snag other auras to get something done, I realize I have to be careful that what I want done is a good thing. It's a lot of responsibility. But the council has already sent notice that they've found someone to teach me to use my Talent wisely. I hope it's someone cute, like Mr. Bindlebrot. Probably, though, it will turn out to be Agatha. Shudder.

Mom and Dad have let me know they're proud of all my hard work. Mom's not working in the library anymore. She says it's because she doesn't want to discourage me from doing my homework research and reading good books. I'm not sure that's true. Lately, she's been spending a lot of time with the head ghost in our house.

I think she may be about to uncover some of the secrets buried in this old place. There's a rumor that if a witch makes friends with a ghost, they'll find out secrets that are not often revealed. Whatever. I'm just glad she isn't at the school, checking books out to my friends. That was just more weirdness than I wanted to deal with.

The only one who isn't impressed by my new Talent is Dorklock. But his girlfriend makes up for that. She thinks I walk on Perrier.

I guess I caved to Dad's notion that friends shouldn't become enemies when I flashed that good luck sign to Maddie. All the anger I had toward her melted away when she flashed one back without a second's hesitation.

I knew things were never going to be the same between us, but that didn't mean I had to give her up as a friend. So I invited her to come out for a visit during school vacation week. Apparently, Armand and her mom had broken up and her mom was going on a singles cruise with some friends. She'd wanted to bring Maddie along (is that weird or what? . . . so Beverly Hills), but she hadn't objected when Maddie asked to visit me instead.

Just as I'd known she would, she loved the turret in my room. It was almost like old times, except that the magic was a lot harder to hide. Mom had to bind Dorklock's powers to get him to stop floating things to freak Maddie out. Fortunately, we didn't need to mind-wipe her. I just explained the house was haunted. She bought it. She's always been a horror movie fan.

She finally even managed to apologize. "I'm sorry about Brent. It was so lame. It's just that you weren't there, and things were really weird with Armand moving in and all."

"The worst thing was that you didn't tell me. Didn't you know I'd give you the 'full steam ahead' sign?" I asked.

"Maybe I was jealous. You'd always had everything, and—" she stopped, as if there were no words.

I stopped the torture. "I get it. I felt that way too. I didn't know about Armand and your mom either."

"It's all good." Especially now that she'd apologized at

last. "I bet you're glad your mom dumped Armand. He seemed like a stinker to me that time I met him." I couldn't resist a bad pun. After all, there was no way Maddie would ever know what I'd done for her. It was just one of those things we couldn't talk about.

"I can't believe you'd forgive me for poaching Brent and lying about it," she said as she painted red stars on my already gold-painted toenails.

"I've learned a lot of things in Salem," I told her. "And mostly I've learned that friends come in all sizes, shapes, and levels of kewl. And they're all valuable, but none of them are perfect." Especially not the mortal friends.

"You've changed a lot, Pru."

"Is that bad?"

"No. It's good. I don't think you would have understood about Armand before."

"Not like I do now. It sucks to have your mother stolen by an alien with a hot bod."

"It does. I think that's why I was so happy to stop talking to you. Your life sounded so great and all."

"Even though I told you I was in some remedial classes?"

She blushed, remembering how she'd served that up to Chezzie. "Man, I was really a beeyotch to you when you so didn't deserve it. I'm glad you guys won Nationals."

"That makes two of us." I couldn't help asking . . . "Was Chezzie spitting fire or what?"

"She said you cheated."

"We didn't."

Maddie looked at me. "I know. And so did Coach—she suspended Chezzie for two games for saying so."

Whoa. That was a cheery thought. My old team *did* remember me fondly—except Chezzie, who probably was more convinced than ever that I was the devil. Oh well, can't win 'em all.

"I wish I could have seen that." I wondered if I could scry it . . . not that I'd do it while Maddie was around. Really talented witches could scry the past as well as the future. I might as well give it a try after Maddie went home.

"I wish you could have too. My closet's still available."

"No. I'm good here. It's only for another year and a half. And I still have to whip the Witches into shape for next year's competitions." I grinned.

Maddie grinned back. "Next year, we might not let you off so easy."

"I guess we'll have to see." Mom had already warned me that I couldn't compete unless I could control my Talent so I didn't use it to unfair advantage against mortals. There was more than a chance that my old team would win. But I was okay with that.

"Until then, though, fill me in. What's up with that geek you used to hang with back when we were texting. Samuel, was it? And how about Daniel?"

"Daniel's gone. He ran away." I shrugged, as if he were old news. "But Samuel's my new BFF."

"You have a guy for a BFF? Isn't that weird?"

"A little. But you'll have to meet him. Then you'll understand."

"Can't wait."

I teased her. "Maybe I should keep him away. After all, you did already poach Brent."

Maddie leaned forward, nearly painting my nose with red nail polish. "I thought this Samuel guy was just a friend."

"He is. He is. Don't go getting your panties in a twist."

She grinned and capped the polish. "I'll see about that. Now I *have* to meet him. If a geek can catch your eye, you've really changed."

I thought about Samuel, and Daniel, and Angelo. And then I thought about all the things To-Do already had scheduled in his little Troll body for me to accomplish. Turning Samuel into boyfriend material would probably qualify as the easiest on the list. "I didn't say he's caught my eye." Exactly. "But you know what the biggest thing living in Salem has taught me?"

"Never count out the geek?" Maddie teased.

I looked around at my room, the room I thought I'd never ever think of as home. "Things change. Sometimes when you least expect it. And almost never the way you were planning for."

About the Author

Kelly McClymer was born in South Carolina, but crossed the Mason-Dixon Line to live in Delaware at age six. After one short stint living in South Carolina during junior high, she has remained above the Line, and now lives in Maine with her husband and three children.

Writing has been Kelly's passion since her sixth grade essay on how not to bake bread earned her an A+. After cleaning up the bread dough that oozed onto the floor, she gave up bread making for good and turned to writing as a creative outlet. A graduate of the University of Delaware (English major, of course), she spends her days writing and teaching writing. Her most recent novels include *The Salem Witch Tryouts*, *Competition's a Witch*, and *Getting to Third Date*, which is part of the Simon Pulse Romantic Comedy line.

Give three cheers for a brand-new series with a ton of spirit!

WANTED

Single Teen Reader in search of a FUN romantic comedy read!

How NOT to Spend Your Senior Year
CAMERON DOKEY

Royally Jacked
NIKI BURNHAM

Ripped at the Seams
NANCY KRULIK

Cupidity
CAROLINE GOODE

Spin Control
NIKI BURNHAM

South Beach Sizzle
SUZANNE WEYN &
DIANA GONZALEZ

She's Got the Beat
NANCY KRULIK

30 Guys in 30 Days
MICOL OSTOW

Animal Attraction
JAMIE PONTI

A Novel Idea
AIMEE FRIEDMAN

Scary Beautiful
NIKI BURNHAM

Getting to Third Date
KELLY McCLYMER

Dancing Queen
ERIN DOWNING

Major Crush
JENNIFER ECHOLS

Do-Over
NIKI BURNHAM

Love Undercover
JO EDWARDS

Prom Crashers
ERIN DOWNING

Gettin' Lucky
MICOL OSTOW

The Boys Next Door
JENNIFER ECHOLS

In the Stars
STACIA DEUTSCH &
RHODY COHON

Available from Simon Pulse Published by Simon & Schuster

"ONCE UPON A TIME"

is timely once again as fresh, quirky heroines breathe life into classic and much-loved characters.

Renowned heroines master newfound destinies, uncovering a unique and original **"happily ever after. . . ."**

BEAUTY SLEEP
Cameron Dokey

MIDNIGHT PEARLS
Debbie Viguié

SNOW
Tracy Lynn

WATER SONG
Suzanne Weyn

THE STORYTELLER'S DAUGHTER
Cameron Dokey

BEFORE MIDNIGHT
Cameron Dokey

GOLDEN
Cameron Dokey

THE ROSE BRIDE
Nancy Holder

From Simon Pulse
Published by Simon & Schuster